Hiya . . .

They say you should write about the things you love . . . and there aren't very many things I love more than chocolate! A couple of years ago I was talking to a friend whose mum had been a chocolate-maker . . . how cool would that be? The idea for the Chocolate Box Girls series started there!

I'd known for a while my readers wanted a series of linked books, so they could get to know the characters and follow their stories into the future. And a series with a chocolatey theme sounded just about perfect to me . . . think of the research I'd need to do! It's a tough job, chocolate-tasting, but someone has to do it . . .

I decided to build the story around five sisters, part of a brand-new stepfamily where the parents have a chocolate business . . . there would be five books, each one told from the viewpoint of a different sister. I've started off with Cherry, a misfit dreamer, always on the edge of things, who suddenly finds herself moving to Somerset to be part of the cool, crazy Tanberry family. Living in a beautiful, crumbling house on a clifftop by the sea is pretty perfect . . . until Cherry falls for her new stepsister's boyfriend, and everything threatens to unravel.

I hope you like *Cherry Crush* . . . the first of the Chocolate Box Girls. It's a story about truth and lies and life on the edge . . . and falling for the wrong boy. What are you waiting for? Unwrap some chocolate, curl up and try a taste of Cherry's story . . . I think you'll like it!

Books by Cathy Cassidy

The Chocolate Box Girls

CHERRY CRUSH
MARSHMALLOW SKYE
SUMMER'S DREAM
BITTERSWEET
COCO CARAMEL

DIZZY
DRIFTWOOD
INDIGO BLUE
SCARLETT
SUNDAE GIRL
LUCKY STAR
GINGERSNAPS
ANGEL CAKE

LETTERS TO CATHY

For younger readers

SHINE ON, DAIZY STAR
DAIZY STAR AND THE PINK GUITAR
STRIKE A POSE, DAIZY STAR
DAIZY STAR, OOH LA LA!

Cathy Cassidy

Cherry Crush

for Beth
Cathy Cassidy

PUFFIN

PUFFIN BOOKS

Published by the Penguin Group
Penguin Books Ltd, 80 Strand, London WC2R 0RL, England
Penguin Group (USA) Inc., 375 Hudson Street, New York, New York 10014, USA
Penguin Group (Canada), 90 Eglinton Avenue East, Suite 700, Toronto, Ontario, Canada M4P 2Y3
(a division of Pearson Penguin Canada Inc.)
Penguin Ireland, 25 St Stephen's Green, Dublin 2, Ireland (a division of Penguin Books Ltd)
Penguin Group (Australia), 250 Camberwell Road, Camberwell, Victoria 3124, Australia
(a division of Pearson Australia Group Pty Ltd)
Penguin Books India Pvt Ltd, 11 Community Centre, Panchsheel Park, New Delhi – 110 017, India
Penguin Group (NZ), 67 Apollo Drive, Rosedale, Auckland 0632, New Zealand
(a division of Pearson New Zealand Ltd)
Penguin Books (South Africa) (Pty) Ltd, 24 Sturdee Avenue, Rosebank, Johannesburg 2196, South Africa

Penguin Books Ltd, Registered Offices: 80 Strand, London WC2R 0RL, England

puffinbooks.com

First published 2010
Published in this edition 2011
010

Set in Baskerville by Palimpsest Book Production Limited, Falkirk, Stirlingshire
Printed in Great Britain by Clays Ltd, St Ives plc

British Library Cataloguing in Publication Data
A CIP catalogue record for this book is available from the British Library

ISBN: 978-0-141-32522-4

www.greenpenguin.co.uk

Thanks . . .

To Liam, Cal and Caitlin as ever, for the love, the laughs and for putting up with me . . . and to Mum, Joan, Andy, Lori and all my fab family, both near and far. Big hugs to all my brilliant friends: Helen, Sheena, Fiona, Mary-Jane, Maggi, Jessie and everyone who has been there for chats, emails, party nights, cakes and hugs . . . you are the best.

Thanks to Catriona for being a perfect PA, Martyn for doing the adding up and Darley and his angels for being all-round brilliant. A special thank you to my lovely editor Amanda for helping me uncover the story I wanted to write, and to Sara for being the best ever cover artist/designer. Thanks also to Adele, Francesca, Emily, Tania, Sarah, Kirsten, Jennie, Jayde, Lisa and the whole brilliant Puffin team, both in the UK and overseas.

Thanks to Sophie, whose tales of a chocolate-making

mum planted the seed of this idea, and to Caitlin, whose love of Japan and all things Japanese helped to shape the story.

Most of all, though, thanks to my readers . . . for making it all worthwhile. You asked for a series, and here it is – hope you like it!

1

There are some things I will miss about Clyde Academy . . . things like macaroni cheese and chips, and syrup pudding with custard, and staring at the back of Ryan Clegg's neck in art class. There are also things I will not miss, like maths tests and school stew, and Kirsty McRae. I won't miss Kirsty McRae at all . . . she and her friends drive me crazy.

They have it all . . . perfect hair with fancy highlights and perfect school uniform, the cool kind that comes from TopShop on Buchanan Street. They get good grades, they're popular, the teachers like them, the boys love them.

Everybody else just wants to BE like them . . . except for me. I am not like Kirsty McRae, not one little bit. I do not have perfect hair, my uniform is second hand and there's a slightly sticky stain on the skirt where I dropped my toast and jam this morning. I don't get good grades, mainly because I do my homework on the bus to school, and teachers don't like me, except for my English teacher, who says I have a very vivid imagination.

I am not totally sure if she means that as a compliment.

I just cannot see the attraction of a girl like Kirsty.

She isn't even nice. When I was seven, I invited her to our flat for tea and she complained that she didn't like bacon butties and asked why our goldfish had a dog's name. I didn't know that Rover was a dog's name, back then. I guess it was Dad's idea of a joke.

Kirsty asked me where my mum was, and I said I didn't have one.

'Don't be silly,' she had insisted. 'Everybody has a mum. Who cooks your tea? Who does the washing and irons your clothes?'

'Dad, of course!'

Well, he didn't iron them, exactly. He just shook things out and laughed and said that a few creases never hurt anyone.

'Are they divorced?' she asked in a whisper. 'Did she run away or something?'

'Of course not!'

Kirsty narrowed her eyes. 'Are you adopted?' she asked. 'Because you don't look anything like your dad! You look . . . I dunno, Chinese, or Japanese, or something.'

'I'm Scottish!' I protested. 'Just like Dad!'

'I don't think he's your dad at all,' she said, and when she saw my eyes brim with tears, she started to smile. When I went back to school on Monday, Kirsty had told everyone I was adopted, and that my dad swept the floor on the production line at the McBean's Chocolate Factory.

He did, sometimes, but still, she said it in a very mean way.

I will not miss Kirsty McRae.

Right on cue, Kirsty flounces into the dinner hall with her little gaggle of friends. They push their way to the front of the queue, then saunter over to the table where I am sitting alone with my macaroni cheese and chips, without even noticing I'm there. They flop down beside me with their plates of salad, flicking their hair and retouching their lipgloss and chattering about boys and dates and nail varnish.

'Hey,' Kirsty says. 'Sorcha, I dare you to chuck a chip at Miss Jardine! Go on, I dare you!'

Sorcha grabs a chip off my plate and flings it through the air. It lands briefly on the head teacher's tweed-suited shoulder and then drops to the ground. Miss Jardine looks round, frowning, and her gaze fixes on me, my forkful of chips and macaroni frozen in mid-air. Her eyes narrow accusingly, but she has no proof and turns back to her dinner. Kirsty collapses into giggles, and I shoot her a frosty look.

'What are you looking at?' she scowls.

'Nothing,' I say, but my mouth twitches into a smile. Kirsty is exactly that . . . nothing.

'Why are you smirking? You are such a freak, Cherry Costello!' Her eyes flicker over me as though I am something small and slimy she has discovered stuck to her lettuce leaf, and for once I dare to meet her gaze. I tilt my chin and smile, and Kirsty's face contorts with fury.

She turns to her friends. 'Hey, did you know Cherry's mum thought she was such a loser that she ditched her and ran off to live on the other side of the world? What does that feel like, Cherry? To know your own mum couldn't be bothered to stick around?'

'You don't know anything about my mum,' I say quietly.

Kirsty laughs. 'Oh yes, I do, Cherry,' she says. 'We were at primary school together, weren't we? Your mum's a film star, isn't she? In Hollywood? That's what you told me in Primary Five. Or maybe she's a fashion designer, living in New York. That was the story when we were in Primary Six. Let's see, what else was there? A model, a singer, a ballet dancer . . . in Tokyo, Sydney, Outer Mongolia. I swear, Cherry Costello, you are such a LIAR!'

Kirsty laughs, and I hate her then, I really, really hate her.

'Leave it, Kirsty,' Cara says, but Kirsty has never known when to leave things. She'd rather poke at them with a sharp stick until they bleed.

'Your mum isn't an actress, is she, Cherry?' Kirsty says spitefully, and the others, even Sorcha and Cara, giggle.

'No,' I whisper, my cheeks burning.

'She isn't a fashion designer either, or a model, or a ballet dancer, is she?'

'No . . .'

It seems to me that the whole dinner hall has gone quiet.

They want to hear what Kirsty has to say. They want to see me crumble.

'They were just stories you made up, Cherry, to make yourself seem more interesting,' Kirsty says. 'Isn't that right? Only it didn't work, because you're not interesting, not one bit. And neither is your mum.'

There's a pain in my chest, the hot, bitter ache of shame. I search around for something to say, a clever quip, a come-back. Nothing. I have used all of my dreams, my fantasies, already, and Kirsty has labelled them as lies. Well, maybe they were, even though a part of me believed them at the time.

'Your mum is probably just a waste of space, like you,' Kirsty says nastily.

I push my chair back roughly, and stand. My legs are wobbly, and my hands shake as I pick up my plate. I should just take my dinner and walk away, to a different table in the furthest corner of the dinner hall, where Kirsty and her crew cannot hurt me.

That's what I should do.

Then again, perhaps it's time I showed Kirsty McRae exactly what I think of her. After all, I have nothing left to lose.

I lift my plate of macaroni cheese and chips and tip it over Kirsty McRae's head, watching the cheesy gloop drip down through her perfectly highlighted hair. Chips roll down her white shirtsleeves, leaving greasy trails, and ketchup spatters her creamy skin like blood.

'Oh. My. God,' Sorcha says.

And, slowly at first, hesitantly, the whole, entire dinner hall begins to clap and cheer.

2

Miss Jardine is not impressed, of course. She doesn't see it as a gesture of heroism, but more of a 'vicious, pre-planned attack on a fellow pupil', which is a bit much in my opinion. I mean, if I'd planned it, I'd have chosen a day when we were having stew or something. Macaroni cheese is one of my favourites.

Still, Miss Jardine is angry, and her lips press together into a line so thin that they almost disappear.

'Poor Kirsty is in the nurse's office, having first aid,' she tells me. 'You are lucky she doesn't have burns, or severe shock!'

I raise an eyebrow. Poor Kirsty? As if. A severe shock might do her good. She could wake up and forget that she'd ever been a mean, spiteful witch. Unlikely, I suppose, but possible.

'Cherry, your behaviour here has been completely unacceptable,' Miss Jardine sniffs. 'What has Kirsty McRae ever done to you?'

I blink. Where do I start? Should I mention the time she flushed my PE socks down the loo, just for a laugh? Or the time she told everyone she'd seen my dad dressed up as a human chocolate bar in Sauchihall Street, handing out free samples of McBean's Taystee Bars?

Should I mention the things she says to other kids, the ones she REALLY doesn't like? Last month, in art, she sliced off Janet McNally's waist-length plait with the paper cutter. She didn't even get into trouble. She claimed she was nowhere near the paper cutter, and somehow Janet got the blame.

Crazy.

'She called me a liar, Miss,' I whisper.

Miss Jardine peers at me over her glasses. 'Liar . . . well, that's a very harsh word,' she says. 'However, a number of teachers and pupils have commented on . . . shall we say . . . your ability to embroider the truth.'

I blink. I think my own head teacher just called me a liar.

'It does seem, Cherry, that you haven't made the best of starts at Clyde Academy,' she continues. 'I have to say, I am a little concerned. I know you've had a rather unconventional childhood, but really, it is no excuse for your tall stories. I understand that last week you told Miss Mercier that you couldn't hand in your art homework because a goat had eaten it. Now, really, Cherry, a goat? In Glasgow? Do you honestly expect us to believe that?'

I honestly do, because it is the truth. We were visiting some old art school friends of Dad's in the Borders that weekend, and I spent over an hour sitting in the sunshine making a careful pencil sketch of Dad's fiddle. I was proud of that drawing. Then, while we were having lunch, next-door's goat got into the garden. It ate my drawing, chewed the corner of the picnic blanket and bit my sunglasses clean in half.

I hope it got indigestion.

'If you tell too many little white lies, Cherry, there will come a point where people will stop listening to you,' Miss Jardine goes on. 'Have you heard the story of the boy who cried wolf?'

'Yes, Miss,' I say tiredly.

She tells me anyway, a yawn-making story about a little boy who tells lies all the time, so that one day, when he sees a wolf and tries to tell his family, nobody believes him at all. The wolf eats him up.

The moral of this story is clear. If I don't stop telling fibs, I may be eaten by a wolf, and it will be nobody's fault but my own.

'The tall stories will have to stop,' she says. 'Before they get any more out of hand. And after the summer holidays, I will arrange weekly sessions for you with the school counsellor. Today's outburst was obviously out of character for you, but it's worrying all the same. We want to help you, Cherry. Not just with the compulsive lying, but with your anger issues.'

A tide of crimson seeps across my cheeks. Compulsive lying? Anger issues? What is Miss Jardine trying to say?

'I won't be here after the summer holidays, Miss,' I say, as politely as I can. 'My dad has fallen in love. He is giving up everything he has so we can live with his new girlfriend in a big house on the edge of a cliff in Somerset. We are going to be a proper family, and we will make a fortune selling luxury, organic chocolates.'

Miss Jardine gives me a long, pitying look.

'Really, Cherry, this is exactly the kind of thing I am talking about!' she sniffs. 'Of course you are not going to live on the edge of a cliff in Somerset! Your father works in McBean's Chocolate Factory, making the Taystee Bars and sorting out the misshapes, which are neither luxury nor organic, and not likely to make anyone's fortune, I think you'll agree. I don't know where you get these flights of fancy from!'

'But, Miss –'

'I think your father would have told us if you were leaving us, don't you?' she says.

My fingers slide over the envelope in my bag. Dad's letter to Miss Jardine has been there for five days now, getting more and more crumpled. There is an orange stain in one corner, where my bottle of Irn-Bru leaked yesterday, and a clot of sticky blue where my biro snapped. There is not much point in handing it over, not when Miss Jardine thinks the whole move-to-a-cliff-edge story is pure fantasy.

Yes, my dad does work in McBean's Chocolate Factory. At least he does for another fortnight, when he'll hang up his apron and collect his last-ever wage packet and his complimentary carrier bag of misshapen Taystee Bars, the ones that somehow missed getting a layer of biscuit or a swirl of white chocolate on top or somehow ended up with a sunken, blobby kind of look. I will miss those bars.

Then we will start packing, dismantling our lives and folding them away into cardboard boxes and bin bags, and we will load our belongings into Dad's red minivan and drive into the sunset. Well, not the sunset exactly, because Dad wants to set off early, but you know what I mean.

We really are going to live on the edge of a cliff in Somerset. Miss Jardine has no idea just how bizarre my life is.

'No more lies, Cherry,' she says.

'Er . . . no, Miss.'

'And of course, I will need you to say sorry to Kirsty McRae.'

'Right,' I say through gritted teeth.

Miss Jardine marches me along to the nurse's office, where Kirsty is curled up on a squashy chair sipping lemonade and eating biscuits. 'Biscuits are very good for shock,' she says, smirking

I don't care, because Kirsty also has traces of macaroni

gloop in her chestnut-and-caramel hair, and a faintly cheesy smell about her. I am mean enough to feel glad about that.

'Cherry has something to say to you, Kirsty,' Miss Jardine says.

Kirsty beams, her eyes bright with triumph.

'I-I'm sorry, Kirsty,' I stammer.

I am not sorry, though, not one little bit. And surely Miss Jardine does not want me to lie about it? I am meant to be turning over a new leaf, being honest and truthful. No more lies.

I look Kirsty McRae in the eye. 'I'm just really sorry that . . . that . . . you're such a nasty, vindictive, SPITEFUL little witch.'

That's when Miss Jardine tells me I am suspended, and on report, and in after-school detention, possibly for the rest of my life.

3

Miss Jardine calls Dad, of course, and tells him everything. She is on that phone to him the minute Dad gets home from work, before he has even had a chance to change. My crimes are clearly too wicked to wait another minute.

I hide behind the kitchen door and listen.

Dad tries to smooth down his sticky-up hair and he shrugs off the McBean's overalls and tries to look as serious as possible as he listens. Miss Jardine has that effect on people.

There are lots of long silences, and lots of sighing. Dad says 'I see,' quite a lot, in a sorrowful kind of way. What is Miss Jardine telling him? That I need to see a counsellor? That I am crazy, violent, living in a fantasy world?

She is the one with the over-active imagination, if you ask me.

Dad flicks on MTV and we sit on the sofa eating beans on toast with misshapen Taystee Bars for afters. Neither of us bothers to take our shoes off.

'Miss Jardine told me you were making up stories again,' Dad says, munching toast. 'Apparently she didn't get my letter explaining the move?'

I bite my lip. 'My pen leaked all over it,' I admit. 'And my Irn-Bru. So I had to explain it out loud. I don't think she believed me. She said that I live in a world of make-believe!'

'Well, don't you?'

I bite back a smile. Dad doesn't like the word 'lies'. Whenever teachers have used it over the years – which they have, quite a few times – he is quick to tell them that I am not a liar, but a skilled and imaginative storyteller, and if they cannot see that then perhaps they need their eyes testing.

It makes me smile, but these days I make a point of keeping Dad away from school parents' evenings, just in case.

It is great to have a dad who believes in you, who backs you up and defends you from mean-faced teachers. It is great to know that Dad thinks I am creative and imaginative, but there is a little voice inside me that wonders if, sometimes, sticking to the truth might just be easier all round.

Stories come easily to me, that's the trouble. A teacher asks me where my history essay is and, right away, a fully formed story pops into my head about how our flat was burgled the night before and my essay was taken away by police detectives as evidence, to be dusted for fingerprints and DNA. I forgot my gym kit, once, and I told the teacher our washing machine had gone wrong, shredding it all into spaghetti-like strips before flooding the kitchen and bringing down the ceiling of the flat below.

It sounds so much better than saying 'I forgot it', so much more interesting and colourful and adventurous. The trouble is, my teachers tend not to agree. They prefer the truth, even if it is dull and grey and boring.

Is it really such a crime, to have a vivid imagination?

'I've explained it all now,' Dad is saying. 'Miss Jardine doesn't think you have settled in too well at Clyde Academy. She says that a fresh start might be for the best.'

'I settled in fine!' I say, outraged.

Well, maybe I didn't . . . but I scraped by, didn't I? Miss Jardine has made it all sound so much worse than it really is, so much more of a big deal. And none of this would have happened at all if it hadn't been for Kirsty, of course.

'She deserved it, anyway,' I say. 'Kirsty McRae.'

Dad raises an eyebrow. 'Is this the same Kirsty who came to tea when you were seven, and ate all the Taystee Bars and made you cry?'

'That's her.'

'Well . . . perhaps,' he sighs.

Kirsty's long-ago visit stirred up a whole lot of trouble, but I was grateful to her too, in a funny way. She made me ask questions I'd never even thought of asking before.

I was seven years old, and I'd never wondered where my mum was, or why I looked so different from Dad or from the other kids at school.

'Am I adopted?' I had asked Dad, a few days later. He'd rolled his eyes and folded me in his arms and wiped my tears away, and later he gave me a photograph of my mum, young and beautiful and laughing, her ink-black

✿✿✿✿✿✿✿✿✿✿✿✿✿✿✿✿✿✿✿✿✿✿✿✿✿✿✿✿✿

hair blowing back in the breeze on the beach at Largs. I was only seven, but I knew even then that I would look just like her, one day. Dark, almond eyes, high cheekbones, skin the colour of milky coffee.

Her name was Kiko and she was Japanese. I was half-Japanese, and I hadn't even known it.

I never missed my mum until I saw that photograph, I swear. Afterwards, though, she was all I could think about. I got books out of the library about Japan. I drew endless felt-pen sketches of dark-haired ladies in kimonos, twirling parasols, even though in the photo my mum was wearing jeans and a jumper. I would imagine pagodas and cherry blossom and brave samurai warriors.

'Are we really leaving Glasgow?' I ask Dad now.

'We really are,' Dad says. 'No more Miss Jardine. No more Kirsty McRae . . .'

I laugh. We clank Coke cans and drink to the future, then Dad tries to flick the TV over to the football, so we wrestle over the remote control and I manage to grab it and chuck it across the room, where it lands with a 'plop' in the goldfish-bowl, with Rover giving it the evil eye.

It starts slowly, the packing up. In the first week of the school holidays, I tidy my room and chuck out a lifetime's supply of broken plastic toys, dusty comics and worn-out plimsolls last seen when I was seven. I sort out a bag of books, two bags of board games and fluffy toys and a bin bag of outgrown clothes for the charity shop. Dad adds a few bags of his own to the haul, chucks the whole lot in the back of the little red minivan and takes a trip to the tip, stopping off at the charity shop on the way.

By the time Dad ticks off his last-ever day at the factory, our flat is starting to look eerily bare. Even my treasures are carefully packed into a big McBean's Taystee Bar box – the kimono, the paper parasol, the fan, the photograph of Mum.

It feels weird, disloyal somehow, packing away my special things. Scary.

'A girl needs a mother,' Mrs Mackie, the old lady next door, used to say. 'Paddy does his best, but . . .' Her voice would trail away sadly.

I told Mrs Mackie that some girls could cope just fine without a mum, look at me and Paddy, after all. I don't think she believed me, and she was right. She knew me a whole lot better than I would ever admit. I wish my mum was still around to say and do all the stuff that mums are supposed to do when their daughters hit their teens, of course I do. An old photo is not much use when you want to ask about periods or bras or boys . . . or why you can never seem to hang on to your friends.

Some things you cannot talk to your dad about.

It's not like I have never wondered what it might be like if Dad met someone special. I'd picture someone pretty and cool who would talk to me about girly, growing-up stuff and take me shopping for shoes and dresses, or maybe someone plump and kind, who'd bake apple pies and hug me when I felt sad. I dreamed up a hundred different versions of the woman who might be my new mum, and pretended to Kirsty McRae that they were real.

A mum was what I wanted, more than anything.

I never realized she might come with strings attached.

4

Dad found Charlotte Tanberry on one of those Internet sites where friends from hundreds of years ago hook up and catch up on what they've been up to. She was an old friend from his art-school days – the days before Mum, before me.

Dad had had big ideas, back then. He wanted to change the world, paint wild, wonderful canvases the size of walls. He has shown me photos of a skinny boy with sticky-up hair and paint-stained fingers, a boy with big dreams.

And Charlotte . . . she'd studied graphic design. Like Dad, she'd never hit the big time – she was divorced and living in Somerset, running her house as a B&B to make ends meet.

Pretty soon, Dad and Charlotte were chatting the whole

time, remembering the old days. Dad was glued to his laptop every evening, flirting and messaging and falling in love.

Charlotte was blonde and pretty, I could see that, but more importantly she looked kind, as if she laughed a lot. She looked like mum material.

'I like her,' I told Dad, and he grinned and said he liked her too. The two of them started meeting up for mushy weekends, sharing hopes and dreams, making plans for the future. I would stay with Mrs Mackie in the flat next door, wishing, hoping, praying things would all work out.

It was a modern romance, an Internet fairy tale.

'Have you ever wondered if there could be more to life than this?' Dad asked, one evening, looking around the dingy flat. 'If you're letting life pass you by?'

I frowned. 'Not really,' I replied.

But things were changing, even though I didn't know it.

Dad worked at McBean's Chocolate Factory because the shift hours fitted perfectly with my school day. I used to think that was cool – I'd seen Johnny Depp in *Charlie and the Chocolate Factory* – but McBean's wasn't much like that, not really. There were no rivers of chocolate, no everlasting gobstoppers. Dad did not get to wear a velvet tailcoat and top hat, just a plastic apron and a hairnet and nasty rubber gloves, and the work was so dull he said it made his brain ache.

One day I came home from school and found him making chocolate truffles at the kitchen table, melting down McBean's Milk Chocolate Bars over a pan of bubbling water on the cooker.

'Don't you get enough of that, at work?' I asked.

'Don't laugh,' he'd answered. 'There's money in chocolate. If an old-fashioned biscuit like the Taystee Bar can sell so well, imagine what you could do at the top end of the market. Handmade, organic truffles, beautifully packaged . . . we could make a fortune!'

I looked at the gloopy mess in the mixing bowl and wasn't quite so sure, but we tried a few, and they tasted a whole lot better than they looked.

The next day, he made another batch, packaged them up in a little card box he'd made and decorated himself, lined with gold tissue paper and tied up with ribbon. He sent them off through the post to Charlotte.

She told him they were fabulous, but Dad said he could do better. He switched from melting down McBean's Milk Chocolate to something more upmarket, and the quality of his kitchen-table truffles began to improve. Some of them were pure brilliant, like the ones with fresh strawberries and cream and the ones with tiny chunks of pineapple and mango.

Charlotte got samples of every batch. It was a long-distance love affair, sweetened by chocolate.

Who could resist?

Charlotte came to Glasgow and the three of us went out on a date, to the park, to the museum, to a Japanese restaurant. Dad wore a new jacket and T-shirt and put gel in his hair to try to tame it. I thought he looked great, my smiley, scruffy, lovely dad, with his rumpled brown hair and laughing blue eyes and his ancient Doc Marten boots that leak in the rain. I guess Charlotte thought so too.

She laughed a lot, and when she couldn't manage the chopsticks at the Japanese restaurant she ended up wearing them in her hair. The three of us stayed up past midnight, squashed on to the sofa drinking mocktails Charlotte had invented out of things like peach juice and

Irn-Bru and pineapple slices. The next day, at the railway station, she hugged me tight, told me to look after Paddy and said that she'd miss me, and I was so happy I felt like I could fly.

So what if Dad was in love? I was too.

'How would you feel,' Dad had asked carefully, 'about leaving Glasgow? Going down to England to live with Charlotte? We could help her run the B&B, and actually get this chocolate business off the ground. And . . . Cherry, we could be a proper family again . . .'

How would I feel? Like all my Christmases and birthdays had been rolled into one.

Only now it's actually happening, I'm not so sure.

What if it doesn't work out the way I've imagined? What if playing happy families is a whole lot harder than it looks?

It doesn't take long to pack the flat up, not once Dad is finished at the factory. The stack of boxes and bin bags by the door gets bigger and bigger. Towards the end of the week, Mrs Mackie comes round, armed with furniture polish and dusters and a mop and a bucket filled to the brim with soapy water. She puts us to work dusting and polishing and mopping the flat, from top to bottom.

'I'll miss you, you know,' she tells us gruffly, as Dad scrubs, scours and bleaches the sink and I polish the taps to a high gleam. 'You were never any trouble, as neighbours.'

'We'll miss you too, Mrs Mackie,' Dad says.

I think of all the times she took me to school because Dad was on early shift, all the times I holed up in her flat eating shortbread biscuits and watching children's TV, waiting for Dad to get home.

Mrs Mackie shakes Dad's hand and presses a warm fifty-pence piece into my palm, and tells me to be a good girl. A sad twist of regret lodges in my chest suddenly, and I want to hug her tight and cry on her shoulder . . . I don't, though. I am trying to be brave. After all, I am getting exactly what I wanted. A mum, a future, the chance to be a family, a chance to be like all the other girls – the Kirsty McRaes of this world. It's just that it feels a whole lot more real, more scary, than I ever imagined . . .

We have been up since six, loading the van, struggling up and down the tenement stairs and out into the lashing rain. Every box, every suitcase and bin bag, is shoe-horned in. Mrs Mackie appears in her nylon housecoat and tartan slippers, and hands us a bag of cheese-spread sandwiches cut into triangles and a couple of slices of fruit cake for the journey. My eyes really do mist over then.

We abandon the brown corduroy sofa, post the keys through the letterbox for the landlord, and by nine o'clock we are on our way.

'I won't miss the rain,' Dad says, trying to be chirpy.

But I think it's raining because we are leaving, because it's the end of something, and the city is sad to see us go.

By eleven, we have covered more than a hundred miles and it is still chucking down. The downpour is starting to feel less like a sad farewell and more like a really, really bad omen. What if this whole move south and find-a-new-family adventure turns out to be a disaster?

I huddle in the passenger seat, holding Rover in his glass bowl, the box of treasures at my feet. My cheek rests against the window, and outside the rain slides down the glass like tears.

'This summer . . . we'll try to see it as a trial,' Dad is saying. 'See whether we can make things work. I think we can, but I want you to know that you come first, whatever happens. If you're not happy . . . if you don't settle . . . well,

we will think again. You're still my number-one girl, Cherry. You know that.'

'I know,' I say softly, but I'm not sure if I do any more, or how long that might last.

Charlotte Tanberry is cool. She laughs a lot, wears chopsticks in her hair, but . . . there is one tiny problem. Charlotte doesn't need a new family because she already has one . . . four bright, beautiful daughters.

I stare out of the window as the little van heads south, leaving Scotland – and life as I know it – behind.

5

It stops raining just north of Preston, and the sun comes out and a big, beautiful arc of rainbow shimmers over the motorway. We stop at a service station for coffee and milk-shake, eating the cheese-spread sandwiches sneakily, under the table of the service station cafe.

I fish around in my bag for the letters sent by Charlotte's daughters, Skye, Summer and Coco, to tell me about them-selves and make me welcome.

Skye's letter is written on black paper in silver gel pen and sprinkled with tiny silver stars; she tells me all about horo-scopes and history and her addiction to jumble-sale dresses. Very odd. Summer's is written in purple on pale pink paper, and her letter is all about ballet and how she dreams of learning to dance *en pointe* and being a prima ballerina one day. The last letter, Coco's, is written in smudgy pencil on a torn bit of paper that looks as though it has fallen in a puddle, or been chewed by a dog, or possibly both. Coco seems to be obsessed with animals and climbing trees, and tells me all about her ambition to have a llama, a donkey and a parrot as pets.

I'm not sure if the letters are comforting, exactly.

Dad has met the girls, of course, a couple of times, on trips down south, but he travelled midweek, using odd days off, and each time I was left in Glasgow with Mrs Mackie. I wish now I'd asked to meet them, once at least.

Coco is the tomboy, he reckons, and Skye and Summer are twins, a year younger than me. There is another sister, Honey, just a few months older than I am. 'Charlotte says that Honey didn't have time to write a letter,' Dad explains. 'She's the eldest, six months older than you . . . she's just finishing Year Nine at the high school. You'll be in the year below her, if everything works out. The younger girls are still at middle school . . . that's the way the system is in Somerset.

'Anyway, Honey's had end-of-term exams to revise for, but I'm sure she's really excited about meeting you. She's very pretty, and clever, and confident . . . I'm sure you'll be great friends!'

'Right,' I say.

'The English school holidays have only just started,' Dad reminds me. 'So you'll have plenty of time to settle in and get to know the girls before you start school. An extra-long holiday . . . brilliant, huh?'

'Yeah . . . brilliant.'

I bite my lip. Dad doesn't understand, really. I am not good at fitting in, making new friends. I am not pretty, or clever, or confident, and Charlotte's children sound all of those things. Being part of a family is way more complicated than I imagined. I never expected sisters to be a part of the deal. Even their names make them sound arty and bohemian and rock-chick-cool.

I can see that I will be the one misshapen Taystee Bar in a family of perfect chocolate-box girls. Great.

It's hours and hours before we finally turn off the M4 to bump along the quiet Exmoor lanes. I am tired and cramped and nervous, and even Rover is looking slightly carsick.

We drive through the pretty village of Kitnor, with its

thatched, whitewashed cottages crowded together along the roadside. The sun is still shining, as if it never does anything else in a place like this.

'Almost there,' Dad says, and panic twists inside me. What if everything I ever wanted turns out to be a disappointment, like a Christmas present you've prodded and dreamed about . . . and then when you open it, turns out it is a handknitted jumper, sludge-green and baggy and slightly lopsided?

I have a few jumpers like that, now that I think about it. Dad is a big fan of charity-shop chic. It has taken me forever to work out what suits me, steering away from the baggy jumpers and finding refuge in primary-coloured skinny jeans and tight cartoon-print T-shirts and plastic bangles, all cheap as chips from Primark or New Look. I will never be a girly girl, but I look OK, except on the days I manage to decorate myself with jam stains or toast crumbs, or splatter my Rocket Dogs with mud.

There's a glimpse of the sea, glinting silver, and then we're driving through steep, thickly wooded hillside. There's a wooden sign jutting out from the hedge that says *Tanglewood House B&B*, and Dad turns the van into a curving driveway fringed with slender, twisty trees and, finally, we're here.

My first glimpse of Tanglewood House takes my breath away. It's big and old and elegant, made from pale golden stone with little arched windows and swooping slated rooftops. There is even a turret, a slim, rounded tower room way up on the second floor, topped with a pointy roof. This house is huge . . . like a house from a fairy tale, where princesses might live. I don't know if I belong in a place like this.

A handpainted banner flutters in the breeze above us, strung from an upstairs window across to one of the trees . . . *Welcome to Tanglewood, Paddy & Cherry.*

'Look!' Dad grins. 'Isn't that great?'

Suddenly the windscreen vanishes, engulfed by a swirl of rainbow-bright fabric, and Dad brakes sharply in a spray of gravel.

'Coco!' a girl's voice yells out. 'Coco, what are you DOING? You've dropped it!'

Dad gets out of the car, and I follow, still hanging on to Rover's fishbowl. A tawny-haired girl in a floppy, green velvet hat is hanging out of an upstairs window, the banner dangling from her hands down on to the van.

'Hello, Skye!' Dad grins. 'Did you paint this? It's brilliant!'

'I've only just finished it,' the girl sighs. 'Coco was supposed to be helping me to hang it up, not drop it right on top of you!'

A second figure, a skinny girl of ten or eleven, still dressed in untidy school uniform, drops down to the ground from her perch in the branches of a tree just to our right. 'Sorry,' she says, all freckles and cheeky grin. 'The string snapped!' She turns away and sprints off through the garden, shouting, 'They're here! They're here!'

The hat girl has vanished, leaving the dangling banner to slither to the floor in a heap.

'Paddy!'

Out of a side door Charlotte comes running, fair hair flying out behind her, laughing, flinging her arms round Dad. He lifts her up and whirls her round and round, the two of them laughing like there is nobody else in the world, for that moment at least.

It makes my tummy flip over.

The hat girl appears in the doorway, arms folded sternly. She is wearing a faded, trailing dress that looks like it came from some ancient dressing-up box, and a pair of weird, strappy shoes that look about a hundred years old. I try not to stare.

'Mu-um!' she huffs, and Charlotte pulls away from Dad, laughing, and hugs me tight.

'Cherry!' Her warm hands squeeze mine and her green eyes shine. 'I can't believe you're finally here! I want you to feel that this is your home too . . . I can see you've met Skye already, and Honey, Summer and Coco can't wait to get to know you too! We've planned a little party, in the garden – nothing fancy, just family and a few friends and some of the B&B guests . . .'

She bends down to scoop up the fallen banner. 'Looks like we weren't quite in time with this,' she grins. 'Never mind . . . Paddy, you'll help me hang it down in the garden, won't you? There's a stepladder just there, against the wall. Skye, you and Cherry can check on the last bits of food for me, and bring them down . . . let's get this party moving!'

Dad shrugs, picks up the stepladder and follows Charlotte off down the garden. I am stranded on the gravel, clutching Rover's bowl. Skye takes it from me and turns back into the house, with me following. 'We've never had a goldfish,' she says. 'We've got a dog, though, and some ducks . . .'

I step into a warm kitchen that smells of sausages and baking. There's a big kitchen table laden with freshly iced chocolate sponge, trifle, cupcakes and strawberry tarts, and a tatty blue dresser with lots of mismatched china, and a pinboard made of real corks, crammed with postcards and little reminder notes. There is even a photo of me and Dad, taken on Charlotte's weekend in Glasgow, and that makes me smile.

Skye puts Rover's bowl down on the dresser and heads straight for the Aga, a big old-fashioned, cream-coloured range cooker, to haul out trays of little sausages and two golden quiches that smell fantastic.

'Here,' she says, handing me a box of cocktail sticks from the dresser drawer. 'Get the sausages speared up. I'll do some tomato and cheese kebabs, because Coco is going through a vegetarian phase. Are you hungry?'

'Starving,' I say.

'Have a sausage,' Skye says. 'Or a cupcake – I won't tell! I didn't think I wanted another sister, but . . . well, I'm glad you're here!'

'I'm glad too,' I say, and I'm surprised to find I mean it. 'Everything's just so . . . well, perfect!'

Skye laughs. 'It's definitely not perfect,' she tells me. 'But hey, it won't take you long to work that out! Who needs perfect, anyhow?'

She takes a tub of glacé cherries from the cupboard and sticks a whole bunch of them round the edges of the iced chocolate cake on the table.

'We made this for you, specially . . . it's a Cherry Chocolate Cola Cake. We sort of made it up.'

'Thank you!' I say. 'It sounds . . . um . . . amazing!'

Skye loads the cakes up on to a wide tray while I try to balance plates of sausages, veggie kebabs and quiche on another, wobbling slightly. 'You'll get used to it,' she says. 'We have to help Mum out with the B&B breakfasts, sometimes.'

As I follow Skye out to the back of the house, I notice strings of fairy lights draped through the trees, and the beat of an old Mika song and the smell of woodsmoke drifting up across the sloping lawn. In the distance, I can see a bunch of people crowded together around a bonfire, talking, laughing, eating. If this is a small party, I'd hate to see a big one.

There are trestle tables draped in bright tablecloths, crowded with food and drink, deckchairs and a patchwork of blankets and cushions scattered across the grass, and there's a shaky figure on a stepladder, fixing the welcome banner to a tree branch. Dad.

I am picking my way carefully across the grass, trying to keep the tray level, when through the trees to my right, I catch a glimpse of something amazing. There's a little oasis of trees, and among the trees, in a clearing, stands a beautiful bow-top gypsy caravan. It looks like something from a storybook, all glossy curves and rich red, yellow and green patterning. A red gingham curtain flutters from the tiny open window. Behind it all, I can see the glint of a stream, curving through the long grass like a silver ribbon.

'Who lives there?' I ask Skye.

'In the old caravan? Nobody. We used it as a den sometimes, when we were kids . . .'

She walks on, but I can't move, can't stop staring at the caravan. I remember seeing one down in the Borders, when I was little and we were staying with Dad's old art school friends. The caravan was parked up beside the road while its owners boiled a kettle over a makeshift campfire and shared out bread and cheese. They looked tanned and tough and slightly scruffy, and the girl had long raggedy hair threaded through with a million different-coloured ribbons. Nearby, a speckled gypsy horse with feathery feet was tethered, eating grass.

Dad said the caravan belonged to New Age travellers, but that not so very long ago real Roma gypsies had lived in caravans like that. They were adventurers, he said, wild and free and romantic.

I thought that the New Age travellers looked wild and free and romantic too, and I told Mrs Mackie about it, once we were home in Glasgow.

'I wouldn't be surprised if there was a little bit of the gypsy in your family,' she told me. 'Paddy's done his share of adventuring, hasn't he? That gap year, or whatever you call it, after art college. Well, of course, it turned into more than a year . . .'

'That's when he met my mum,' I said. 'Maybe she had a little bit of the gypsy in her, as well?'

Mrs Mackie said that she didn't know about that, but she sang me a sad, old-fashioned song about a girl who ran off with the raggle-taggle gypsies, and I liked that. I used to wonder if my mum had run away with the gypsies too. Why not? It was just as likely as the other stories I imagined.

And now I have walked into a whole new life, a life that seems too good, too perfect to be true. A new mum, a proper house, a bunch of brand-new sisters, a beach . . . and a gypsy caravan in the garden. I can't stop grinning.

It can't get any better than this . . . can it?

6

Well, maybe it can.

Suddenly, out of the trees, a big, fluffy dog appears, circling me, pawing me, jumping about. 'Hey, hey!' I laugh. 'Stop that!'

But the dog won't stop. I think it wants food, because its wet nose keeps nudging my leg, my elbow, the tray itself. I hold the tray high, but still the dog is dancing round me, and then my foot lands on something soft and fluffy and the dog yelps and I scream, and the whole tray of quiche and sausages and veggie kebabs goes flying into the air.

'Whoa, there . . .'

I'm about to go flying myself, when someone catches my arm. Suddenly I am leaning against a boy who smells of woodsmoke and ocean, a boy whose arms fold me close then push me back again so that we're blinking at each other in the fading sunshine.

'Are you OK?'

'I . . . I think so!'

How could I be anything else, when a boy with suntanned skin and sea-green eyes and hair the colour of wheat is holding me? He looks cool, with skinny jeans and a tight blue T-shirt and a baggy black beanie hat balanced carefully on the back of his head, even though it is July.

I catch my breath and wait for him to pull me close again, but he doesn't, of course. He just grins and looks at me for a long moment, until I swear I will melt.

'You've got to be Cherry, right?' he says. 'I'm Shay Fletcher.'

'Shay . . .' The name falls off my tongue like a spell, a wish.

Then I notice the dog, hoovering up quiche and sausages from the grass, his tail wagging madly, and I don't know whether to laugh or cry.

'It's the sausages,' Shay tells me. 'He's mad for them. Bad boy, Fred!'

I drop down to my hands and knees in the grass, scrabbling for plates and dishes.

'I can't believe I dropped them. Charlotte trusted me, and now . . .'

'Blame the dog,' Shay says. 'He's a maniac, Charlotte knows that. Seriously, it's no big deal – nobody will mind.'

I gather up the dishes and the tray and turn back towards the house, leaving Fred to hoover up the evidence. Shay is at my side. 'I said I'd get some logs for the bonfire,' he explains.

'Right,' I say. 'So, you are . . .?'

'Me? I'm nobody,' Shay laughs. 'I'm not family or anything, if that's what you mean. I live down in the village, go to the high school with Honey . . . and you, now, according to Charlotte. I've known the Tanberrys for years.'

We slip into the kitchen through the side door, and I stack the plates and dishes next to the old ceramic sink.

'You're not a bit like I imagined you'd be,' Shay says. 'I've met Paddy before, the last time he was down, and I suppose I thought you'd look like him, but . . .'

'I don't look anything like him,' I grin. 'I know. My mum was Japanese.'

'Wow! How cool is that?'

'Well, she hasn't been around for a while,' I say.

Shay looks dismayed. 'No . . . um . . . obviously. I'm sorry. I mean . . . well, I'd better just shut up, right? I just meant . . . well, you look really cute and your accent is great, and . . . no, I really am shutting up now. Ignore me! Let's get those logs.'

I follow him outside. I cannot believe that a boy has just told me I am cute. Cute? Me? Shay Fletcher may be the only boy alive who thinks so.

My heart is thumping. I have had a million crushes on cool boys, but never, ever, has a boy liked *me*. Boys always seem to like the confident, popular girls, girls like Kirsty McRae. They never see me as interesting, attractive. Except possibly Scott Pickles who used to live in the flat downstairs, and that doesn't count because he is only seven, and pretty short-sighted.

Shay is different. He is way, way out of my league, but I am pretty sure his eyesight is OK. And he is looking at me intently, with an ocean-coloured gaze that takes my breath away.

Shay loads me up with branches and logs from the

woodpile by the gable end. I end up with twigs in my hair, and he picks them out, gently. 'You'd better tell me everything,' he says, smiling. 'Your whole life story, from start to finish. Then I'll tell you mine, or play the guitar for you . . . deal?'

'Deal,' I whisper.

I think I would tell Shay Fletcher anything, any time, always. I would carry logs for him, to the ends of the earth, and wear twigs in my hair every day just so he could pick them out again.

Shay grabs an armful of logs himself, and leads the way down the lawn towards the party, the bonfire. People turn as we approach, so many smiling faces, and I'm smiling too, because my heart feels full of hope that this is really where I'm meant to be – this is the place where I belong.

'Hello, Cherry! Welcome to Kitnor! We've heard so much about you . . .'

'It's great to meet you at last . . .'

Charlotte appears through the crowd of strangers, smiling. 'Cherry! Has that wretched dog been hassling you?' she asks. 'He just ran through here with half a quiche in his mouth . . .'

'I think I stepped on him . . . I dropped the tray . . . I'm sorry!'

'No, no, Fred's a brute, I should have warned you . . .'

I'm right beside the bonfire, in the middle of the party, with the fairy lights flickering overhead. Shay lets the logs and branches slide out of his arms to make a new woodpile, and I do the same, watching the flames light up his face with flashes of orange and gold. He steps in behind me, his fingers brushing my arm, and his touch burns right through my sleeve and into my skin, like fire.

Skye and Coco are in front of me, grinning, and a girl who looks exactly like Skye only glossier, somehow, and minus the floppy hat and the funny, trailing dress. Her clothes are a dozen different shades of pink, and she moves gracefully, like a dancer.

I remember that Skye and Summer are twins, but I have never seen two girls so alike and so different, both at the same time.

'It's OK,' she says, laughing at my confusion. 'I'm Summer . . . if in doubt, remember I wouldn't be seen dead in droopy hats and jumble-sale dresses!'

Skye swats her with a red-checked napkin, rolling her eyes.

'So, I guess the only one of us you haven't met yet is Honey . . .'

The eldest Tanberry sister is sitting on a fallen tree trunk, a glossy blue guitar at her side, waist-length hair the colour of sunshine tumbling around her shoulders. She is chatting to a bunch of teenagers, laughing.

Dad said she was six months older than me, but Honey Tanberry might as well come from a different world. She's pretty, a whole lot prettier than Kirsty McRae. She could be a model or a singer or a teen movie star, with her little blue-print dress and her polka-dot hairband. She could be anything she wanted to be.

A prickle of anxiety runs along my spine. Girls like Honey, like Kirsty, never like me, no matter how hard I try. They are the popular girls, the cool girls, and I don't fit into their world. Honey isn't going to be my friend, though – she's going to be family. That's different, surely?

I hope.

Honey glances over, and her smile fades. She stands up slowly, her smoky-blue eyes looking me up and down, unimpressed. I cannot work out why she's so frosty, but I know I'm not imagining it. When her lips curl into a grin, I shiver.

Shay drops my elbow and steps away from me, as if I have suddenly become contagious.

'I'm Honey,' the girl says, and her arm snakes round Shay's waist, reeling him in and holding on tight. 'You've met Shay then? My boyfriend?'

I look at Shay, and his gaze slides away from mine, guilty, awkward. I am invisible again.

'Looks like it,' I say.

'OK,' she says, fixing me with an arctic glare. 'Good.'

Dreams of family, dreams of friendship, dreams of love – abruptly, they all crash and burn, falling in little pieces around me, sharp and bright and painful, like broken glass.

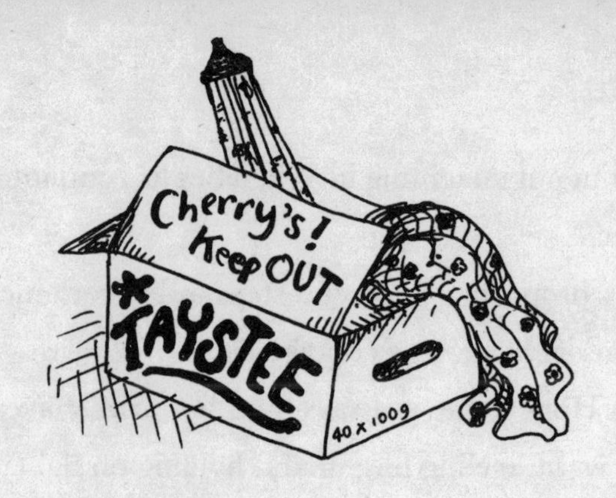

7

I am hiding under the duvet, which is crisp and ironed and smells of washing powder, unlike my duvet from home, which was always crumpled and bobbly and littered with toast crumbs. The pillow under my head is squashy and feather-filled, and even the mattress is springy and soft, with no dodgy springs poking me in the ribs in the middle of the night.

I should be happy, but I am not.

I don't belong here. My dreams shattered the minute I met Honey Tanberry, the minute Shay Fletcher turned away from me as if I didn't exist.

I had to grit my teeth and smile my way through the party, and I told about a million lies.

'Yes, I'm so excited to be here!'

'Yes, everyone's been so welcoming! I can't wait to get to know you all a bit better . . .'

Surprise surprise, Honey and Shay didn't come anywhere near me all night. They wrapped their arms round each other and laughed and whispered until I felt so sick of them both I could have screamed.

I didn't, though. It wouldn't have been fair on Dad and Charlotte. I ate a slice of Cherry Chocolate Cola Cake and it was surprisingly good.

I kept smiling, even when my face felt frozen, and I kept saying the right things, the polite things, the positive things. I let Skye and Summer show me the gypsy caravan, the silver stream. I followed Coco down the steep path that leads down from the garden to the beach, and my feet sank into damp sand as I looked out across the glinting ocean, beautiful, silent, still.

When it got dark, Shay Fletcher picked up the blue guitar and started to play, and, of course, Dad fetched his fiddle from the minivan and the two of them played sad songs around the bonfire, under the stars. It was probably the best party I had ever been to, and the worst.

And then, at the end of the evening, when the guests

had gone and we were walking back up to the house, they dropped the bombshell.

I would have to share a room. I've never done that before – our tenement flat may have been grey and scruffy, but it had two bedrooms. You'd think, in a house this big, you could get a bit of privacy . . . but no. I am sharing a room, because, of course, Tanglewood House is a B&B and that means that the family are squished into little attic rooms while the paying guests take all the posh bedrooms.

Guess who I get to share with? Not Skye, because she already shares with her twin, Summer. Not Coco, because she has the box room and it's only just about big enough to fit in a single bed. And that leaves . . . Honey.

Yippee.

It was the turret room, of course, and Honey was the princess. What did that make me? The servant-girl step-sister who got to sleep in the cinders?

Honey must have known about the plan, but she looked even more disgusted than me at the whole idea of it. She locked herself in the bathroom for a late-night shower while I hauled a bag of clothes and my treasure box up the stairs, ditched them at the end of the bed and dived under the duvet in my T-shirt and knickers. I heard her swear under her breath when she came back in, but I wasn't sticking my head above that duvet, not for anyone.

Now, though, I have no choice. I cannot stay curled under a duvet for the rest of my life, although right now it seems very tempting. The turret bedroom is silent. Before that there was a flurry of huffing and sighing and drawers being opened and shut and the sound of things being sprayed and scooshed.

I think it's safe. I think Honey is up and away.

I lift a corner of the duvet and peer out, and sure enough the coast is clear. I get up quickly, grab sky-blue jeans, a clean top and undies, and pad to the bathroom to wash. My face in the mirror looks sad and tired, my black fringe sticking up at an angle. I drag on my clothes and creep back across the landing.

When I push open the bedroom door, I see Honey sitting at her dressing table, wearing the pink silk kimono from my treasure box and painting her eyelids turquoise.

'Don't you ever knock?' she asks.

Fury rises in me like a fever. The pink kimono is one of the few things I have that are special, one of the few things

that links me to my mum. I can see that Honey has rummaged through the rest of the box as well, leaving the Japanese fan and the paper parasol abandoned on her duvet.

'Don't you ever ask, Honey?' I counter. 'Don't you ever think of asking, before you take other people's things?'

'This is *my* room,' she snaps. 'If you leave stuff lying around, what do you expect?'

'I didn't leave it lying around!'

She raises one perfect eyebrow in the mirror. 'Sharing a room wasn't my idea, OK?' she snarls.

'I kind of guessed that . . .'

I don't think Honey would want to share anything with me, unless it was the swine-flu virus, or possibly the plague. The feeling is mutual, but she doesn't want the kimono, I know, she is just trying to wind me up, get a reaction. Why give her the satisfaction? I take a deep breath.

'Shay told me you were flirting with him last night,' she goes on. 'I mean, seriously – don't go there, Cherry. He is way out of your league.'

Flirting with Shay? As if! No, he was the one flirting with me, I am certain of it. The boy must have an ego the size of the Exmoor National Park to go telling his girlfriend I was chasing him. OK, I might have been interested, for about a split second, but he is Honey's boy, and obviously, that makes him out of bounds. I just wish someone had told him that, before he went messing with my hopes and dreams.

'You must think you're so clever,' Honey says. 'You and your waster dad. One minute you're stuck in a Glasgow slum, eating reject chocolate bars, and the next you're moving in on us . . .'

I blink. Glasgow slum? Waster dad? If there was a plate of macaroni cheese and chips handy right now, Honey would be wearing it.

'You're crazy,' I tell her. 'We've turned our lives upside down, given up everything to come here. It's not easy to leave all your friends behind . . .'

Well, it wouldn't be, if I actually had any. Honey doesn't know that, of course . . .

'And for the record, there is no way I'd be interested in your boyfriend,' I go on. 'I've got one back home, and he's way better-looking than Shay Fletcher. I'm missing him like mad already . . .'

✿✿✿✿✿✿✿✿✿✿✿✿✿✿✿✿✿✿✿✿✿✿✿✿✿✿

Honey smiles, as if she can see right through the lie.

'Boyfriend?' she asks. 'What's his name?'

I cast around for inspiration, but all I can come up with is an image of Scott Pickles, the little boy from the flat downstairs back home.

'Scott,' I say. 'His name is Scott. And for your information, Honey, Glasgow is the coolest city in the world. We had this massive apartment with . . . with . . . balconies, and a spiral staircase, and a roof garden . . .'

Honey raises an eyebrow, amused, and I realize, too late, that Dad has probably told the Tanberry family all about our little tenement flat in the West End. And Charlotte, of course, has actually been there.

I try again. 'My dad had a good job –'

'At a chocolate factory, yeah, I heard,' Honey says, stroking eyeliner pencil beneath first one eye, then the other.

My cheeks burn, and I long to wipe the smirk off Honey's face.

'That's right,' I say brightly. 'He was a manager at McBean's, in charge of . . . um . . . research . . . and quality control. He was one of the top men. He practically ran the place . . .'

Honey laughs. 'And now he's here . . . with no job at all, right? How convenient!'

'You're twisting things!' I argue. 'Dad's going to help Charlotte with the B&B, and they're going to go into business together making handmade, luxury chocolates –'

'Using whose cash?' Honey counters, turning round to face me properly. 'Let's see, it would have to be Mum's, because from what I've been told, your dad hasn't a penny to his name. Face it, Cherry, he's a liar and a chancer . . . and you are too. There was no luxury apartment, and there was no manager's job . . . and I have my doubts about the boyfriend too. Who are you trying to kid? Seriously, Cherry, don't even go there. You may have fooled my mum and my sisters, but you don't fool me!'

'I'm not trying to fool anyone! We've been alone, just me and Dad, for years and years –'

'Oh, spare me the sob story!' she cuts in. 'I'm not going to fall for it. My mum might not be able to see it, but I am wise to you. Just listen, OK? I don't want another sister, because I have three already, and trust me, that is more than enough. And I don't want your dad around either, because you know what? I already have a dad. He's smart and cool and he loves me . . . and he loves Mum too, actually. I know he does. So don't think for a minute that you can worm your way in here and make yourself at home, because he will be back one day, I promise you that. And then where will you be? Nowhere!'

Nowhere – or anywhere – would be better than being here with Honey Tanberry.

Wishes don't always come true. Why did I ever think it could be that easy? Wherever I am, whatever I do, there will always be a mean girl stirring up trouble, trying to spoil it for me.

What is it about me they find so unappealing? I have been trying to work that out for years. The teen mags always tell you to 'just be yourself' and let new friends come to you, but seriously, they don't know what they are talking about. Girls like Honey and Kirsty McRae look at me and see the human version of a reject Taystee Bar, a girl who has missed out on a few vital layers from the production line of life.

I've tried to add in those missing layers, with bright, glam stories of my missing mum, designed to make my life look at least a little more interesting. It doesn't work, of course.

I grab the cardboard box with shaking hands and repack the parasol and the fan.

'These things are special,' I tell her, my voice wobbling.

Honey sighs and shrugs off the kimono, scrunching it into a ball before throwing it at me. 'You didn't think I really wanted it, did you?' she laughs. 'As if. Moth-eaten tat is really not my style.'

Tears sting my eyes. 'What is your problem, Honey? What have I ever done to you?'

'You're here,' she snaps. 'You're here, and you shouldn't be, OK?'

Her blue eyes flash and her lips curl into a smile like ice. She wrenches the treasure box from my hands, yanks open the little arched window and tips the whole lot out into the bright July morning.

'Get out, Cherry Costello!' Honey whispers. 'Don't you know when you're not wanted?'

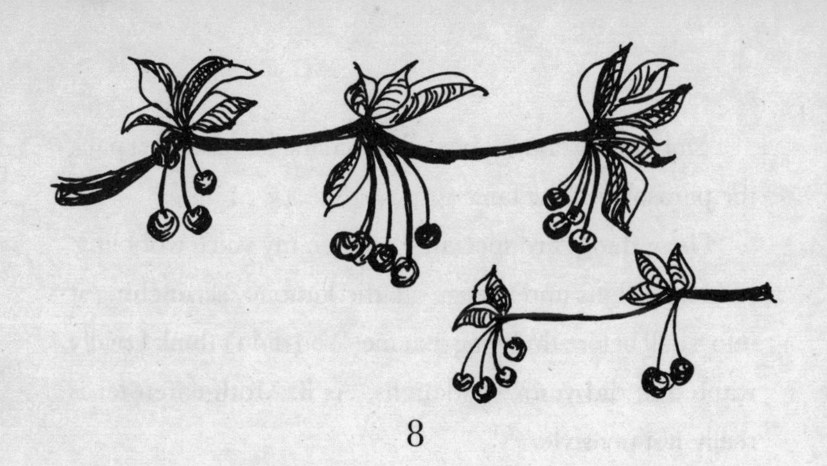

8

As fallouts go, it is pretty spectacular.

The pink silk kimono flutters like a banner from the tree near the window, and the Japanese fan is perched in its branches like a rare and exotic bird. The paper parasol lies half-open on the grass, lifting slightly in the breeze, and the framed photo of my mum lies face down on the gravel.

Dad and Charlotte stand on the driveway, arms folded, faces stern.

'Honey?' Charlotte shouts up at the turret window. 'Cherry? What is going on? Come down here right now!'

Honey flings me a look of total disgust, and flounces down the stairs and out into the sunshine, leaving me to trail along, stunned, in her wake.

✿✿✿✿✿✿✿✿✿✿✿✿✿✿✿✿✿✿✿✿✿✿✿✿✿✿✿✿✿✿✿✿

'Do you have an explanation?' Charlotte asks as the two of us emerge on to the gravel driveway. 'Honey? Is this something to do with you?'

'As if,' she says carelessly, and I want to slap her. 'The box must have fallen off the window sill.'

'Cherry?' Charlotte looks at me, frowning. 'That's not what happened, surely?'

I glance at Honey, and her eyebrows flicker upwards, daring me to drop her in it.

'Must have been,' I shrug.

'Have you two argued?' Dad demands. 'Is there something going on here?'

'Like what?' Honey asks, all innocence.

'It's nothing, Dad,' I tell him, and watch the anxiety fade from his eyes as he exchanges glances with Charlotte.

'Well . . . just be more careful, next time,' Charlotte tells Honey. 'You have to respect other people's possessions when you're sharing a room . . .'

Honey rolls her eyes. 'I don't want to share a room,' she whines. 'Mum, please . . . it's nothing against Cherry, obviously, but . . . well, we're teenagers! We need our space!'

'Honey, sweetheart, it's not that simple . . .'

Coco climbs into the tree to rescue the Japanese fan and Skye tugs at the hem of the pink kimono until it falls into her arms. Summer picks up the paper parasol, twirling it a little. I reach down to get the framed photo, wincing as I see the broken glass.

'I'll get you another frame,' Dad promises, and packs the cardboard box up carefully and carries it back inside.

Charlotte takes Honey in too, still arguing that she needs her own room, and it really isn't fair to make her share, not when she is trying so hard already to adjust. Nobody asks what I think, but then, I am the outsider here, aren't I?

'Don't take it personally,' Summer says. 'Honey is very possessive about her room. Maybe you could share with us?'

'It'd be a bit of a squash,' Skye considers. 'But we wouldn't mind.'

'I don't want to cause any trouble,' I say.

'You won't! Take no notice of Honey, really,' Coco says. 'She's just a bit . . . well, moody, these days. It's best to ignore her.'

✿✿✿✿✿✿✿✿✿✿✿✿✿✿✿✿✿✿✿✿✿✿✿✿✿✿

'Mum says she's going through a phase,' Skye shrugs. 'A very long phase.'

'She's very sensitive,' Summer says. 'She's still getting over our dad leaving.'

'I wish she'd hurry up then,' Skye huffs. 'He's been gone three years.'

I try for a smile. Three out of four Tanberry sisters seem to like me . . . that's something, I guess.

'I love that kimono, Cherry,' Skye is saying. 'Where did you get it?'

'It was my mum's,' I say softly, and the three girls open their eyes wide. I have their interest now, and their sympathy. 'That and the photo and the parasol and the fan . . . well, they're all I have left of her.'

'Seriously?' Coco breathes. 'Oh, wow!'

'So tragic,' Summer says.

'Did they really fall off the window sill?' Skye wants to know.

I roll my eyes. 'What do you think?'

'We know there is a problem,' Charlotte tells me, later on, in the kitchen. 'We know you don't want to stir up trouble,

Cherry, but . . . well, Honey has been having a hard time, these last few years. She misses her dad.'

'Right.'

'I really thought it would be good for the two of you to share a room.' Charlotte frowns. 'I think, though, at the moment, she might prefer to have her own space . . .'

'I'm sure you'd like your own space too,' Dad says. 'But there aren't any other rooms, and the guest bedrooms are all full, so we wondered . . .'

'We don't want you to feel excluded . . .'

'There are other options . . . it was just a thought . . .'

'What?' I ask, exasperated.

'Well. How would you feel,' Charlotte asks, 'about sleeping in the gypsy caravan?'

'Outside?' I say.

'Well, yes, but it is July, so you won't freeze, and we could rig up electricity and heating, and move it closer to the house, and if you're worried about security, the dog could sleep in there with you –'

'No!' I interrupt. 'I like it where it is. I mean . . . I *love* it, where it is. And I don't mind about the dog, but . . . oh, Charlotte, I'd love to sleep there! Can I really?'

I fling my arms round Dad's neck and Charlotte laughs and joins us in a three-way hug, and it's all settled.

I guess every cloud has a silver lining, and this one is extra shiny. I move my stuff in right away. My clothes fold away into drawers under the bed, my books line up on the shelf, and Rover's bowl fits perfectly on top of the brightly painted cupboard. Charlotte has washed and ironed the pink silk kimono after its adventure in the tree, and shows me how to slide a length of bamboo cane through the sleeves to hang it from the caravan wall, draping the fabric to one side so you can see the print of cherry blossom.

Skye helps me to arrange the Japanese fan and the paper parasol, and Dad has been down to the village for a new photo frame, so Mum's picture is as good as new.

I'd like to say it felt like home, but my room at home was a mess, a black hole with peeling wallpaper and torn posters. Empty plates and toast crumbs and chocolate wrappers and crumpled clothes littered the carpet. I once lost a Rocket Dog pump in there for six whole months.

The caravan under the trees feels a million times better.

It is perfect, with bright, curving walls and clever

cupboards patterned with swooping birds with flowers in their beaks. Charlotte has aired the mattress, put on fresh sheets, brought down the duvet from last night and tucked a patchwork quilt over the top in case it gets cold. There is a soft, fluffy rug on the floor, and Dad has drilled a hole in the doorframe and run a lead through, so I have fairy lights inside the caravan as well as strung through the trees outside.

'It seems right, somehow,' Charlotte says. 'Cherry sleeping under the cherry trees!'

That's when I look up through the dappled branches and see that the trees that arch above the gypsy caravan are laden with dark, glossy crimson cherries. My heart flips over. Real cherries, growing on real cherry trees . . . that's something you don't see very much in Glasgow.

Dad puts the stepladder against a tree and picks me a bowlful of cherries, and I sit on the caravan steps in the sunshine, letting the little bursts of sweetness explode on my tongue.

I remember eating cherries once with Mrs Mackie from next door, and she showed me a rhyme where you count the cherry pits and look into the future to foresee who your true love might be. I line up the cherry pits carefully and recite the rhyme she taught me. *Tinker, tailor, soldier, sailor, rich man, poor man, beggar man, thief . . .*

It comes out as thief, which either means Shay Fletcher, who has stolen my heart, or possibly that I will fall in love with a no-good waster. Shay Fletcher again, obviously.

Except that I won't. He may have fooled me for a minute or two, but Shay Fletcher is bad news. He was out of bounds the whole time, yet he flirted with me and then had the cheek to tell Honey it was the other way round. I chuck a bunch of cherry pits into the long grass and count again. *Tinker, tailor, soldier, sailor . . .*

I should be safe enough with that. Sailors are kind of thin on the ground these days. Maybe the whole cherry-pit rhyme needs updating?

'Been playing house?' Honey comments, as I walk back up to the house for tea, but I just smile to myself and pretend she doesn't exist.

After we've eaten, Summer, Skye and Coco walk me down to the caravan with tin mugs of cold, fizzy Irn-Bru. We sit on the caravan steps, with Fred curled beneath us on the grass, and sip our drinks and talk about how weird it will be to be stepsisters.

'Are you missing your friends?' Coco wants to know. 'It must be hard, moving to the other end of the country and leaving them all behind. I wouldn't like it.'

'Um . . . well, I'm trying to see it as an adventure,' I say. 'But I am missing my friends, of course . . .'

What friends? I close my mouth before any more lies can seep out. Telling stories has only ever landed me in trouble, but at least this one sounds plausible. Most people have friends, right? It's just me who doesn't.

'You can keep in touch,' Summer suggests helpfully. 'There's always texts and email and MSN. And I suppose your very best friends could always come down and visit you . . .'

'Yeah . . . I'm sure they will . . .' I trail away into silence. 'We had lots of plans . . .'

Like that is ever going to happen.

'I'm more worried about making new friends, really,' I say, and that much, at least, is true.

'Oh, that'll be easy,' Skye says dismissively. 'Everyone will like you, don't worry!'

'Honey doesn't,' I hear myself say.

'Don't worry about Honey,' Coco tells me. 'She'll get used to it in the end.'

'I hope so,' Summer sighs. 'I hate it when she's all moody and stroppy.'

'I know,' Skye says. 'I can understand her being upset when Dad left – we all were. Then there was the divorce, and that wasn't easy, I suppose. It was the end of things. But seriously, when she heard about you and Paddy –'

'Shhh,' Coco says, and Summer and Skye look slightly shifty.

'I suppose we were all a bit wary,' Summer admits. 'We'd met Paddy, and we knew we liked him, but a new sister . . .'

'We weren't sure what you'd be like . . .' Skye ventures.

'We didn't know if we'd get on with you!' Coco admits.

My fingers tremble, curled round the tin mug, and the sweet Irn-Bru tastes sour on my tongue.

Then Skye reaches out and tugs at my hair, grinning, and the fear falls away again. 'But we do like you,' she tells me. 'You're . . . well, really different! Really cool! Honey said you might be pushy and moody, and try to take over . . . but you're not like that at all. And I actually think it's a good thing you're here, whatever Honey says, because she will have to wake up now and let go of the past, move on. Things are changing, and I think that's a good thing!'

'D'you think so?' I ask.

'Definitely,' Skye nods.

'Me too,' Summer says.

'And me,' Coco chips in. 'So . . . do you think they're going to get married? Paddy and Mum?'

I almost choke on a mouthful of Irn-Bru.

Marriage? It's not that I haven't imagined that for Dad, but things are moving so fast right now I am not sure I am ready to think about it happening for real. Dreams and reality are very different things, as I'm finding out. I have dreamed of having a mum for the longest time, but I never imagined having to share one with four other daughters, and I definitely never thought about the fact I'd have to share Dad.

I imagine a pretty, country church and Charlotte in a white dress and Dad in a suit that doesn't quite fit. I imagine squirming in a flouncy frock in icing-sugar shades, alongside Skye, Summer and Coco, the four of us smiling for the camera behind our posies of flowers. Then I picture Honey, and the image shatters abruptly.

Skye and Summer exchange glances.

'Get married . . .' Skye says carefully. 'That's a big step . . . I don't think Mum's planning to do anything in a hurry. I think she just wants to see how this goes, first . . . if things work out.'

'They will, though,' Coco insists. 'Won't they? I think it'd be great to have a dad again. Paddy could teach me the violin –'

'No, he *couldn't*!' Summer yelps. 'It was bad enough when you were learning to play the recorder! Honestly!'

Coco rolls her eyes, impatiently.

'Well, I think it'd be cool,' she huffs. 'We'd be proper stepsisters then.'

'But . . . Dad and Charlotte have both been married already,' I explain. 'To other people. They probably want to take things slowly. Make sure everything's right . . .'

I don't say it, but I'm not sure if Dad and Charlotte are the ones who need time to adjust. I think it's us who need time to adapt. A wedding? I don't think I can see that happening, not for a while.

'It might be cool,' Summer says apologetically.

'Definitely,' Skye agrees. 'But not yet. Let's just wait and see.'

'Let's just get to know each other, first,' I chip in, and Coco sighs.

Later, Dad and Charlotte come down with logs from the woodpile, and Dad builds a little bonfire and we sit around it on the grass. Dad plays his fiddle in the fading light.

Above us the trees rustle gently in the breeze, and the stars come out in a velvet sky.

9

Next morning, Fred wakes me up with a frenzy of barking and tail wagging. I pull back the curtain and peer through the caravan window, and there is Dad looking bright and smiley, picking his way across the grass with a tray laden with breakfast treats. He is wearing a blue collarless shirt with the sleeves rolled up, along with his charity-shop skinny jeans, and his hair is sticking up a little as if he has not long stepped out of the shower.

We have only been in Somerset a couple of days, but already Dad looks younger, more relaxed than I have seen him in years. I open the door and sit down on the step with the quilt wrapped round me, and Fred streaks past me, jumping up at Dad, his tail waving madly.

Dad laughs and swats Fred away. 'No sausages, silly

dog . . .' he tells him. 'Did you sleep OK, Cherry? Were you warm enough?'

'I slept fine,' I say. 'I was really toasty, and Fred curled up on the end of the bed like a big fluffy hot-water bottle.'

Dad sets the tray down on the dew-damp grass and spreads a picnic blanket, and after a few curious sniffs to make sure there are no sausages to be had, Fred abandons us and trots off up to the house in search of breakfast. His loss. The tray is loaded up with orange juice and yoghurt and hot chocolate, and Dad hands me a plate laden with fresh pancakes and maple syrup, possibly the best breakfast ever invented.

'Don't be getting ideas,' Dad tells me. 'This won't happen every day, but I thought, just this once . . . to celebrate your first night in the caravan. Besides, I wanted to show Charlotte my pancake skills. I think she is impressed!'

A smile tugs at my lips. 'Of course she is,' I tell him. 'You are the pancake king of Glasgow. Well, of Kitnor, now!'

'My fry-up skills are pretty legendary too,' Dad says. 'Charlotte says I can have a try at doing the guest breakfasts without her tomorrow . . . with Skye and Summer to help out, just until I get the hang of it . . .'

'Don't worry,' I tell him. 'You'll be brilliant. Just stay calm and if anything goes wrong, add on a side order of pancakes. They'll be eating out of your hand!'

'I wish,' Dad says. 'With some people, it takes a bit more than pancakes . . .'

He sighs and takes a slurp of hot chocolate, and I wonder if he was really fooled by Honey's Little Miss Innocent act yesterday.

'It's all a bit frantic, isn't it?' he goes on. 'And the guests are the least of it! I feel like I haven't had a chance to talk to you properly since we got here, and I wanted to make sure you were OK.'

'I'm OK,' I promise. 'It's a bit like being thrown in at the deep end, but . . . Skye and Summer and Coco are really nice . . . and Charlotte is lovely, obviously, but . . .'

'. . . but?' Dad echoes.

I sigh. 'Well, I'm not sure Honey is mad about having us here,' I say carefully. 'She seems a bit . . . prickly?'

Dad nods. 'Just a bit. I had an idea that something wasn't right, yesterday, but I didn't want to make a big scene, for Charlotte's sake . . . I think we will have to tread carefully with Honey.'

I sigh. Tread carefully is right . . . I have a feeling that life with Honey will be like picking your way through a minefield. There could be explosions at any minute.

'She's not a happy girl,' he says. 'Charlotte knows she's struggling, but she's turned a blind eye for a while, thinking it would help. I guess she's been hoping Honey will snap out of it, put the past behind her . . . Well, maybe she will . . .'

Dad frowns, looking into the distance, as if at something just out of reach.

'I suppose I'm saying that I know Honey might try to make things difficult,' he says. 'Just be careful, and try to remember she's not quite as tough as she seems. OK?'

'OK.'

'It's going to be fine, Cherry,' Dad grins. 'This is such a huge change, for both of us, and for Charlotte and the girls too. I'm not saying it will be easy, but I know we can make this work. I never imagined I'd get another chance to be happy . . . well, you know, the way I was happy with your mum. I've always wanted to be able to give you a proper family, and now I think maybe I can . . .

'I want you to be as happy here as I am,' he goes on. 'It's the start of something wonderful, I know it is. Charlotte and I . . . we've been friends for a long time, so we know each other well. To find each other again, to fall in love . . . it's more than I could have hoped for. We share so many dreams, so many interests. We can work together, not just on the B&B, but on the chocolate business too.

'I've done a lot of research and I'm certain we can make it work. Charlotte's going to design a website, put together an image, and once I have all my facts and figures sorted I'll put together a proposal for the bank, see if we can get a business loan. It's exciting!'

Dad looks so happy, so hopeful, that I fling my arms round him and hug him tight, so tight I can smell pancakes and maple syrup on his breath, and the gentle waft of lime-scented shower gel.

There is nobody in the world I love more than my dad. I want him to be happy, because he deserves to be, after years of slogging away on the production line at the McBean's Chocolate Factory, years of making the best of things, of eating misshapen Taystee Bars and beans on toast, of watching MTV with me while the world passed him by. Well, not any more.

'It's time to live the dream,' Dad says. 'It's not easy to join together two families, but it can be done, and I think it will be worth all the effort. Charlotte and I so want it to work . . .'

'I know,' I say, and I can't keep the smile from my voice. I want to be a part of this family too. Charlotte . . . the Tanberry sisters . . . Tanglewood House . . . all of them are a million times more amazing than anything I ever dreamed of, because they're real. I never imagined someone like Honey in the picture, of course, but in the bright light of morning I wonder if I am worrying too much about her. She saw me talking to Shay, and if he told her I'd been flirting with him – well, no wonder she got the wrong end of the stick.

Shay is probably the kind of fickle, flirty boy who chats up any female between the ages of five and fifty. That would be enough to make anyone mad, but I am not interested in Shay Fletcher, not one bit. I expect he is the kind of boy who likes to keep a whole bunch of girls dangling, his own personal fan club. I for one do not want to be a part of it.

Honey will see that, and slowly she will realize that I am not a bad person, and that Dad is cool and kind and good stepdad material. We can make the jigsaw pieces fit after all . . . maybe.

'I want it to work too,' I whisper. 'More than anything . . .'

'Well then,' Dad says. 'We'll have to make it, won't we?'

It feels like a pact, a promise.

10

The week unfolds, and slowly I get used to the caravan, used to Tanglewood. I wake early, when the sun streams through the red-and-white checked curtains, and read or draw or dream.

By nine I am usually up at the house, washed and dressed and eating a DIY breakfast of toast and marmalade with Skye, Summer and Coco, while Dad and Charlotte run around frying bacon and poaching eggs for the guests. It is always kind of frantic, and one of the sisters is always pressed into service as waitress, taking trays of eggs Benedict or grilled kippers to the holidaymakers eating in the big, airy conservatory dining room.

Honey never appears for breakfast, which suits me just fine, and for the first few days I just hang around Tanglewood with Skye and Summer and Coco. We help Charlotte make beds and hoover and clean the guest bedrooms, and it's fun because we are all doing it together, dancing around to the radio and chasing each other with feather dusters.

Later, we laze in the garden, sunbathing, reading, talking, and again, Honey never joins us. Sometimes she goes out to see friends in the village, but mostly she stays in her room.

Often, when I look up at the turret room, the little arched window is open, and I can just see Honey, sitting on the window seat with a sketchbook on her lap, her long hair lifting softly on the breeze. Sometimes she wears it braided into a thick, long plait, like Rapunzel from the big book of fairy tales Mrs Mackie gave me once for Christmas.

Charlotte finds a hammock in the attic while she's sorting out a space for Dad's stuff, and we string it up between two trees and take it in turns lying in the shade, trailing a hand through the grass. Coco introduces me to the ducks, three oil-black runners who are tall and elegant and upright, as if someone has stretched them out of shape somehow. We feed them cornmeal and watch them splash and swim on the pond in their enclosure.

'Your fish might like it in there,' Coco suggests. 'More room.'

'Noooo – the ducks might eat him,' I tell her. 'Rover is fine where he is, really.'

'I'd like some fish,' Coco says thoughtfully. 'And a llama and a donkey and a parrot, of course. Mum says we can't afford more pets, but I'm going to be a vet one day, so I could look after them all.'

'I think you'd make a great vet,' I say.

'Well, it's not definite yet,' she frowns. 'I might decide to work for Greenpeace instead, and go all around the world in that boat they have with the rainbow on, and save the whales and the rainforest and stuff . . .'

'Sounds good,' I tell her. 'If anyone can do it, you can.'

Coco looks up at me through a tangle of tawny, bird's-nest hair. 'Nobody else believes me,' she says, and her blue eyes are serious. 'But I am going to do something amazing, one day. I know I am!'

'I believe you,' I say.

Coco grins. 'I'm glad you're here,' she says, and I'm glad too.

Midweek, Skye takes me on a guided tour of Kitnor. We

walk down from the house, along the twisty, narrow lane that winds through the wooded hillside and dips down at last towards the village. It is the kind of village I didn't think existed outside storybooks, with an old-fashioned baker's shop and a butcher's and a deli and a greengrocer's, as well as a supermarket and a newsagent and a whole bunch of cafes, pubs and B&Bs.

'It's a real tourist place,' Skye explains. 'But it's cool too.'

Skye is still wearing her velvet hat, and yet another jumble-sale dress, but nobody gives her a second glance, so I am guessing this is her usual style.

'That's the bookshop,' Skye chats on. 'And that's the hardware store – the old guy who runs it still sells tin buckets and fly papers and brushes to sweep a chimney with. It's really mad. And that's the post office, if you want to get some postcards for your friends.'

'Oh . . . maybe,' I say. 'I've been meaning to do that . . .'

Inside, I grab a couple of postcards of thatched cottages, to keep Skye quiet. I can send one to Mrs Mackie, at least.

'Hello, Skye,' the lady behind the counter beams. 'Enjoying the school holidays?'

'Yes, Mrs Lee,' Skye says.

'And who is your lovely friend?' the woman continues, smiling at me. 'Not local, I think. And perhaps more than a friend – family, maybe? Although I must say you don't really look alike . . .'

The woman peers at me, frowning. She flicks back her dark wavy hair, and her silver hoop earrings jangle.

Skye laughs. 'Mrs Lee has gypsy blood,' she tells me. 'She can see things . . .'

I think of the gypsy caravan I saw years ago in the Borders, and the one I am sleeping in now, and Mrs Mackie's song and her theory that Dad has a little bit of the gypsy in him.

I blink. 'See things?'

'Sense things,' the woman says. 'I can see beneath the surface, to the truth of things . . .'

I feel myself shrink away, like a kid caught with her hand in the cookie jar, but Skye doesn't notice. 'You're right, as usual, Mrs Lee,' she says. 'This is Cherry, my new stepsister. Well, kind of. She and her dad, Paddy, have just come to live here. Isn't that cool?'

I hand over the thatched cottage postcards and Mrs Lee takes them, flipping my hand over gently to see the palm.

'A girl at the crossroads,' she says. 'A new family, truth and lies, a make-or-break time . . . difficult choices, Cherry.'

Right now, if I had the choice, I would be a million miles from here. This woman is clearly nuts.

'Um . . . two second-class stamps, please,' I say.

Mrs Lee smiles. 'Of course. I hope you settle in well, pet!'

I smile through gritted teeth and follow Skye back out into the sunshine.

'She's a bit odd,' Skye says. 'But quite cool too, if you like that sort of thing. She once told me to beware of strangers and not to let a love of history go to my head, and that exact same day I ended up getting a detention off this new supply teacher for wearing a floppy vintage sunhat in class . . .'

'Er . . . right . . .'

'Anyway . . . that's the church, over there, it's twelfth century . . . ' Skye chats on. 'And that's the primary school, and I can show you the park . . .'

A posse of little kids on bikes swerve past us in a skid of gravel, all asking Skye if she's coming to the park, and we end up following them over and going on the swings, the slide and the roundabout. I haven't done that since I was about eight years old, seriously. The kids try to talk us into a game of footy, but Skye says we are too busy right now, and drags me off for more sightseeing.

I now know where the allotments are, and the community centre, and even the bottle banks and the public loos. I have been introduced to about a million people, beaming middle-aged ladies and whiskery old men and tribes of little kids with skipping ropes, and all of them know Skye and clearly think she's wonderful. I am beginning to agree – Skye's enthusiasm is infectious.

'Fancy a milkshake?' Skye asks, tugging me towards a cafe called The Mad Hatter. 'This is where we always go, they do amazing banana milkshakes and the best cream scones in the village . . .'

We push through the door and my heart begins to race – Honey and Shay are holed up in a corner booth, sipping Coke and chatting. I try not to smile, not to blush, not to care.

'Hey, Skye, Cherry!' Shay calls, grinning and waving. 'Over here!'

I catch Shay's eye and turn away, coldly, pretending to look at my postcards.

'You can have our seats,' Honey says to Skye. 'We were just going.'

Shay blinks. 'We were?'

'We were. C'mon, Shay, I'm not hanging around here to talk about dolls and ponies with my little sister and her freaky friend . . .'

I feel like I've been slapped, and a tide of crimson floods my cheeks.

'Miaow,' Shay says to Honey. 'Finished your saucer of milk, have you?'

'I'm surprised she hasn't curdled it,' Skye is saying, elbowing her way into the booth. 'Honestly, Honey, like we'd want to hang out with you anyway.'

Shay picks up his blue guitar and slings it over one shoulder, adjusting his slouchy black beanie hat. Honey just flicks her waist-length hair and slicks on another coat of shimmery lipgloss while she waits.

'See you around,' Skye says.

'Not if we see you first,' Honey says sweetly, and Shay just shrugs apologetically and herds her out of the cafe.

'She doesn't mean it,' Skye tells me, as the door jangles shut. 'Well, she does, but it's nothing personal. She was meant to be going up to London this weekend, to see Dad . . . only he rang last night and cancelled it. Again. D'you remember, just after tea, when Mum was on the phone for ages and she told us to go outside and not bother clearing the dishes away?'

I nod slowly, remembering Charlotte's face, tired and weary, as she held the phone and ushered us outside.

'So Honey's extra prickly, right now,' Skye says. 'Dad's useless, only she can't see that . . .'

'Oh . . . right,' I whisper. 'I'm sorry . . .'

Skye shrugs. 'Don't be. He was never much of a dad at the best of times. He means well, but . . . he's pretty selfish, really. And he was awful to Mum. He's never once been back to see us here. He was meant to come and stay for the weekend, that time Mum went up to Glasgow to stay with you and Paddy, but he cancelled at the last minute and a friend of Mum's had to come over instead.'

I open my mouth and close it again, speechless.

'Remember what you said the day you first got here, about everything being perfect?' Skye says. 'Well, I guess you can see now that it isn't. It's a long way from that.

Honey's angry with everyone, all mixed up – it's like living with a thundercloud, sometimes. Mum's scared to say anything to her, half the time. I think it's great that you and Paddy are here . . . things will have to change now.'

I bite my lip.

'I hope so, anyhow,' Skye sighs. 'Because I am majorly fed up with Honey lately. Thank goodness she's got Shay, because he's the only one she really listens to. He's good for her. He's really calmed her down. I don't know where he gets the patience, because she's always so moody and mean . . . but I think she really loves Shay.'

A little knife twists in my heart, but I ignore it. This is not what I wanted to hear.

'They make a good couple,' Skye chatters on. 'They're both good-looking, and popular, and cool . . . I'd love to have a boyfriend like Shay one day!'

'I don't like him,' I say.

Skye blinks. 'What? You don't like Shay?' she echoes. 'But everyone likes him! He's great, really sweet and kind. He spends so much time up at our place it's like he's some kind of adopted brother . . .'

Perfect. That's all I need.

'He's one of the family, really,' Skye ploughs on. 'You'll like him, once you get to know him.'

'I don't think so,' I say stubbornly. 'He seems kind of . . . shallow. And vain. Why wear a beanie hat in July? And I bet he uses straighteners on that fringe.'

'Probably,' Skye agrees. 'So what?'

I roll my eyes. 'I just don't like boys like that. You know, trailing round the whole time with that blue guitar, playing at being a rock star . . .'

'No,' Skye corrects me. 'He can really play – you heard him, at the bonfire party. Seriously, Cherry, give him a chance. Shay is OK.'

The waitress comes over to take our order. Skye switches on a smile and launches into her introduction spiel, and the waitress grins and says she hopes I'll be very happy here, and lets us have our banana milkshakes and cream scones for free.

Skye decides that we should walk back to Tanglewood House along the beach, so we wander down through Kitnor Quay, past round-bellied fishing boats and shiny-sleek yachts moored up along the jetties, and a row of neat little sailing dinghies, hauled up on the grass.

'That's where Shay lives,' she tells me, nodding towards a pretty thatched cottage next to some converted outbuildings on the quayside. 'His dad runs the sailing centre – Shay works there too, in the holidays. He must have had an afternoon off, today. They teach kids to sail, run outward-bound courses, hire out dinghies and banana boats to the grockles –'

'Grockles? What are they?'

'Tourists!' Skye explains. 'It's what we call them down here. There are always a few, no matter what the time of year, but now that the holidays have started they'll be everywhere. Having picnics in the fields, lying around on the beach, clogging up the tea rooms . . . of course, we need them, so I'm not complaining. Just about every business in Kitnor needs the grockles to survive. The B&B will be packed out all summer . . .'

I take a look back at the cottage and the outbuildings, noticing the sign that says *Kitnor Sailing Centre* and the canoes and paddles stacked up against a whitewashed wall. Shay does not look like a sporty kind of a boy. I cannot imagine him hauling in sails and lugging trailers about and kitting out plump, middle-aged grockles with wetsuits and luminous orange life jackets, but I remember that he smelled of the ocean, and now I know why.

Tinker, tailor, soldier, sailor . . .

Is there no escape from this boy?

Although if Shay is working at the sailing centre all summer, he won't have time to hang around Tanglewood House. I hope.

Skye is back in tour-guide mode. She slips an arm through mine as we walk, telling me about smugglers' caves and ruined castles and the archaeologists who sometimes come to this bit of coast to hunt for fossils and dinosaur bones.

'I found a fossil once,' she says, eyes shining. 'I bent down to pick up some shells . . . I saw something half-buried in the sand, and it turned out to be an ammonite!'

'A . . . what?'

'It's the fossil of this spiral-shaped sea creature,' Skye explains. 'They lived millions of years ago, and now they are extinct. And I had one in my hand, can you imagine that? I mean, this little creature used to swim in the sea, right here, back when dinosaurs roamed the earth. It was like being given my own little piece of history!'

'Awesome,' I say.

Skye grins. 'It was,' she says. 'Not everyone understands about history. Summer and Coco and Honey all think it's boring, just dusty relics and stuffy museums. But history isn't dull, it's brilliant. Just look at the name . . . history . . . it's all about stories!'

'Kings and queens and smugglers,' I say. 'Mystery and drama and intrigue and adventure . . .'

'Exactly!'

Skye doesn't know it, of course, but I am an expert at storytelling. Other people have a whole stash of memories to dip into, but I have hardly any . . . no happy families stuff, nothing except Dad and me and a past that neither of us want to look back at. Stories help to fill the empty space where my mum should be. I have rewritten history so many times in my own head, I don't even know the truth any more. Does it even matter?

I think it does. It's pointless to tell Honey I used to live in a big, swish apartment if she knows I didn't, and even telling Skye, Summer and Coco I had tons of friends back in Glasgow is kind of risky. Besides, if the Tanberrys aren't perfect, maybe I don't have to be, either?

Maybe it's time to leave the stories for English lessons.

I want to be a part of this family, and if that means keeping my mouth closed when the lies unfurl on my tongue, then that's what I will have to do.

I am not going to do anything to mess this up.

I think of the spirally little sea creature drifting around in a long-ago ocean, and I can't help smiling.

We walk on, making plans for the summer, plans that involve swimming in the sea and going for long bike rides and picnics, and checking out cute grockle boys in the village. We walk right round the bay and past the headland, until we are in the little cove beneath the cliff path that leads back up to Tanglewood House.

Suddenly, Skye ducks away from me, running right down to the water's edge. 'So . . . swimming in the sea, right?' she challenges.

She kicks off her shoes and socks, pulls the trailing dress up over her head, ditches it on the damp sand and sprints into the surf wearing a purple vest and knickers. 'Come on!' she yells, kicking up a spray of silver. 'It's fantastic! Hardly cold at all!'

Yeah, right. It may be July, but this is not the Mediterranean. Against my better judgement, I kick off my shoes, peel off my socks. The damp sand makes me shiver.

'Come on, Cherry!' Skye laughs. 'I dare you!'

That's all it takes. I wriggle out of my jeans and run into the sea in my T-shirt and knickers, and as soon as that first wave hits me I am screaming, because the water is not cold, it is icy, arctic, agonizingly freezing. Skye grabs on to me so that I can't retreat, and the two of us jump and hop and screech with laughter as the tide breaks over us.

I'm not sure if Skye feels like a sister yet, but she is starting to feel like a friend.

11

On Friday evening, I am sitting at the kitchen table, writing my postcard for Mrs Mackie and pretending it's for a friend who is actually under sixty years old. I shield the card with my hand while Charlotte dishes out plates of pasta and pesto with garlic bread.

'Where's Honey?' she asks. 'I called her ten minutes ago!'

'I think she's in her room,' Summer shrugs. 'She's turning into a hermit, lately.'

Settling in well, I write on the postcard. *The house is beautiful and we are right by the beach, so I can swim whenever I want to. I am sleeping in a real gypsy caravan, along with Rover and a dog called Fred. Everyone is really nice . . .*

Well, almost everyone is really nice. It's not a lie, exactly.

Already Mrs Mackie is fading into the past, along with

the brown corduroy sofa and Clyde Academy and Kirsty McRae. Who needs Kirsty, anyway, when you've got Honey Tanberry? She goes straight in at number one in my top-ten list of Mean Girls I Have Known.

I sign my name and slip the postcard into a pocket to post next time I am down in the village.

'Honey!' Charlotte calls up the stairway. 'Tea's ready!'

She shakes her head and hands out plates of pasta.

'We might as well make a start,' she says. 'If we wait for her, it'll go cold . . .'

A few minutes later Honey slopes into the kitchen looking deathly pale, with blue shadows beneath her eyes and grey-tinged lips. She looks like a ghost-girl.

'Are you feeling OK?' Dad asks, and Honey scowls.

'It's make-up,' she says. 'Obviously.'

'Looks like Halloween's come early,' Charlotte sighs. 'What's the story, Honey?'

'A few of us are going down to Georgia's to watch the *Twilight* DVDs,' Honey says. 'We thought it'd be fun to dress up a bit.'

'OK,' Charlotte says. 'Sounds good. Sit down, love, get your pasta while it's hot.'

Honey curls her lip. 'We're having pizza at Georgia's,' she says carelessly. 'So I'll give this a miss, if that's OK. Don't wait up for me . . .'

Charlotte frowns. 'But . . . you love pasta and pesto!' she argues. 'And I've made garlic bread specially, with cheese grated on, the way you like it . . .'

'Too bad.'

Dad and Charlotte exchange glances, and then Charlotte sighs, her shoulders slumping. 'Don't be too late then. Your curfew's eleven. And don't go scaring any small children!'

'As if,' Honey huffs, stalking away with her black velvet dress swishing, slamming the door behind her.

'My sister, the vampire,' Summer smirks.

'Bet she's meeting Shay,' Coco adds. 'She might kiss him. I bet that's why she didn't want garlic bread.'

A piece of crust sticks in my throat and makes me cough, and Dad has to pat me on the back and Coco fetches me a glass of water.

Skye grins. 'Love at first bite . . .'

I wake in the dark, my heart racing, with someone banging on the caravan door. Fred is growling, a low, angry rumble that flares into a yelping bark. For a moment, I can't work out where I am, or why, and then I remember and wish I hadn't, because I am on my own in a caravan in the middle of nowhere, with a growling, fluffy dog and an axe-murderer trying to get in.

'Cherry!' a voice calls, and I almost jump out of my skin. 'Cherry! It's me! Open up!'

I switch on the fairy lights and lift the curtain on the door, and outside I see a shadowy figure in a werewolf mask with a dramatic fall of scratchy grey hair, a blue guitar slung over his shoulder.

Not an axe-murderer then.

I unlatch the door and Fred launches himself out into the darkness. There's a muffled yelp and the twang of a mangled guitar string, and when I peer out Shay Fletcher is sprawled on the grass, his werewolf mask askew, with Fred licking him half to death.

'Fred!' he huffs. 'Get off!'

The fluffy dog jumps back into the caravan and hides behind my legs. I can see he would be a great asset in the event of a real axe-murderer turning up unannounced. Shay Fletcher grins at me. 'Did I scare you?' he asks.

'Too right,' I scowl. 'Put the mask back on, quick.'

'Hey,' he says. 'That's harsh. I was just passing, and I thought I'd say hi . . .' He gets to his feet, grinning, brushing down his jeans.

I huddle on the steps in my patchwork quilt, and Shay settles himself on a fallen log.

Even in the twinkling light from the treetop fairy lights, I can see that I was right about Shay Fletcher. He is not crush material. Some people might fall for the floppy, wheat-gold hair, the freckled nose, the grin . . . me, I am not impressed. Well, only a little bit.

Besides, he has terrible taste in girlfriends.

'Are you mad at me?' Shay asks.

'Why would I be mad? Because you turn up unannounced in the middle of the night, trying to scare me to death? Because your girlfriend is the meanest girl alive? Or because you told her I was flirting with you, the other night, at the bonfire party?'

'Flirting? I didn't say that.' He frowns. 'Where did you get that idea?'

'Let me think . . .' I consider. 'Yup . . . that would be from Honey.'

Shay looks puzzled. 'I never said anything like that, honest. You can flirt with me any time you like . . .'

'You're funny,' I snap.

'I like to think so. No, I just wondered if you were hacked off with me. You blanked me at the cafe.'

'You were busy,' I sigh. 'With your girlfriend.'

'Listen, I just wanted to say that maybe Honey is being a little bit less than welcoming right now,' Shay says. 'But she'll get over it, and anyhow, it doesn't mean we can't be friends. I promised to play my guitar for you . . .'

My heart leaps, then plummets again as I remember the things Skye said about Shay and Honey.

He's good for her.

I think she really loves Shay.

Great.

'I'll let you off that promise,' I tell him. 'That was before I knew you were going out with my new stepsister. So . . . does she know you're here?'

'Well, no, but . . .'

I bite my lip. 'Shay, why *are* you here?'

He grins, and it lights up the darkness better than the fairy lights. He is shallow and fickle and a born flirt, but still, it is hard not to like Shay Fletcher, just a tiny bit.

'Like I said, we can be mates, can't we?' Shay frowns. 'You were going to tell me the story of your life.'

'It's almost midnight . . .'

He pulls a face. 'So? You weren't asleep, were you?'

'Of course not,' I bluff.

'Well then. Like I said, I just happened to be passing!'

'Yeah, right,' I sigh. 'The *Twilight* fancy-dress thing. I think I prefer vampires . . .'

'Bad choice,' Shay says. 'Why fall for a boy who glitters in the dark and flies you to the top of a tree for a first date? Everyone's gonna be a letdown after that. No, you'd be better off with a werewolf. Perfectly behaved, except on full moons. So . . . what'll it be? Trick or treat?'

'It's July,' I tell him. 'Halloween is months away, and I'm all out of treats . . .'

'Tell me a story then,' Shay says, sitting down on the fallen tree trunk. 'Tell me about you.'

I sigh, exasperated. This boy could wear down a stone. 'If I tell you, will you go away?'

'If you want me to,' Shay shrugs, and I feel myself

weaken. Talking to him, telling him a bit about my past . . . would that be a bad thing, as long as it shut him up and made him go away?

'I want you to.'

I put an arm round Fred and lean my cheek against his fur, searching my mind for the right place to start. I could tell Shay anything, after all. It doesn't have to be the truth. Does it?

'Once upon a time . . .' he prompts, and I sigh and take up the story from there.

'Once upon a time there was a young man named Paddy who wanted to paint the world with rainbow colours,' I begin. 'When he left art college he went travelling, and met a beautiful Japanese girl called Kiko. They fell in love and travelled the world and all the colours of the rainbow followed after them . . .'

'I'm liking it,' Shay tells me. 'Where do you come in?'

'I'm getting to that bit! After a while, they discovered they were having a baby. They settled down in a *minka* house in Kyoto with rice-paper walls and *tatami* mats on the floor, and when their baby was born they named her Sakura, because it was cherry-blossom time and soft-pink flowers hung heavy on trees all around the city . . .'

'Hang on,' Shay interrupts again. 'Who is this Sakura person?'

I put a finger to my lips.

'So the little girl, whose name meant *cherry blossom*, grew bigger and stronger, and all the colours of the rainbow danced when she laughed. She knew she would always be safe and loved, as long as her mum and dad were there at her side.

'One day, at cherry-blossom time, Sakura and her mum went down to the park to look at the trees, and a brisk north wind tugged the blossoms from the branches and they drifted to the ground like snow. Sakura started to cry, but her mum hugged her tight and told her not to be sad, because life was just like the cherry blossoms, beautiful but quickly gone, and the trick was to enjoy the beauty of it while you could, to make every second count . . .'

Shay has started playing his guitar, a soft, sad tune I've never heard before. It drifts through the night like a memory. My voice wobbles a little and I glance at Shay, his face lit up by the twinkling fairy lights, listening.

'A few months after that, Sakura woke one morning and her mum was gone. And all the colour had gone out of her world, and nothing was ever the same again . . .'

A tear slides down my cheek, and I blot it with Fred's fur. The past is full of long-buried feelings. I have never shared those memories, those feelings, with anyone before – not even Dad. I glance at Shay and look away again, quickly. What is it with this boy that makes me dare to show him the things I've kept locked inside for so long?

He puts his guitar down.

'Oh, Cherry,' he says quietly. 'Sakura – she's you, right?'

'You have to go now,' I tell him. 'You promised . . .'

'But the rest of the story!' he protests. 'What happened to Sakura's mum? Where did she go? What happened next?'

I shake my head. I am stepping into dangerous territory, and it scares me.

'Just go, OK? Please. And stay away, Shay. You shouldn't even be here.'

He stands up, shivering, slides the guitar strap over his shoulder. 'I'm sorry, Cherry,' he says. 'About everything.'

He pulls on the werewolf mask and walks away.

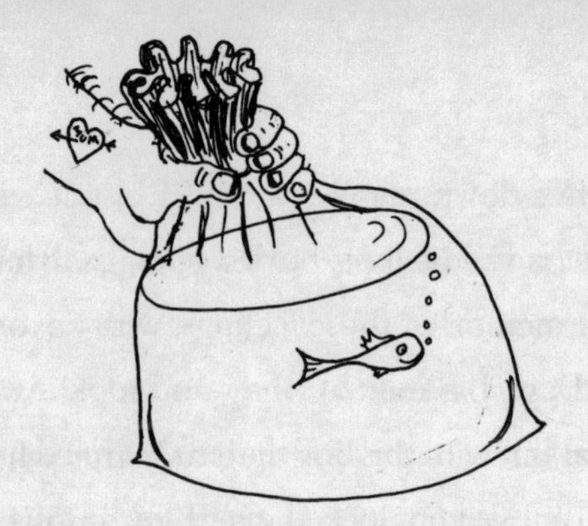

12

I sleep late, and when I wake my lashes are damp with tears. The past is a dangerous place. You can go there in a story, make it seem softer, sweeter, than it really was . . . but then you sleep and the truth seeps out without you even knowing, and you wake up feeling sour.

I have a lazy breakfast of chocolate and banana, and pad across to the hammock with Rover, in his shiny glass bowl, in my arms. As the hammock sways, the water in the bowl laps gently against the glass and Rover gives me a dark, reproachful look. Perhaps he's seasick?

Maybe Coco is right, and he would like a bigger space to swim around in. I imagine a pond, calm and sleek and beautiful, with a little Japanese-style bridge and water lilies and a stone pagoda.

That might be quite cool.

I lower the bowl down into the long grass and gaze down at him with a sigh.

Rover and I go back a long way.

I won him on a fairground stall at Largs when I was seven years old, flinging ping-pong balls into shiny fish-bowls. I was trying to win this huge pink teddy bear with a red satin bow, but I didn't stand a chance. I made Dad pay for five goes, but I think that in the end the kid on the stall got fed up with us and handed over a fish just to make us go away.

When I saw Rover, a sliver of orange-gold beauty flitting about in a plastic drawstring bag full of water, I forgot all about the pink teddy bear.

Dad chose the name, of course. He said Rover was a great name for a pet, and that maybe we could train him to fetch sticks and guard the flat for us, and it took me a little while to realize he was joking about that. Kirsty McRae put me straight, there, of course.

Rover had to live in the big enamel soup pan to begin with, but on pay day Dad took me to the pet shop on Byres Road and bought a big shiny glass bowl with a water filter and a bit of plastic weed and a little stone archway to swim in and out of.

I fed him every day, just a pinch of reddish-brown flakes, and Rover would stop whatever he was doing and fly up to the surface in a split second to eat. I cleaned the water every week, using a soup ladle to empty the dirty water without disturbing him.

I had a library book on looking after goldfish. I took it very seriously.

It sounds crazy, but I used to tell Rover everything. It said in my library book that goldfish had very short memories, like three seconds or something. That was how come they didn't get bored swimming round and round in circles, apparently, but I wasn't convinced. Rover looked kind of bored to me.

But it was safe to spill my secrets, either way, and if I sometimes got sad, then that was OK too, because Rover would forget it all in three seconds flat, so I never had to feel bad for making him miserable. I was always very careful not to drip tears into the bowl, because goldfish do not like saltwater.

'Shay Fletcher is bad news,' I tell Rover now, in a whisper. 'He is off-limits.'

Rover flicks his tail.

'He belongs to someone else. Someone who hates me . . .'

Rover darts through the little stone archway and does a quick slalom run in and out of the plastic weed.

'But . . . I can't stop thinking about him. I really like him. Is that wrong?'

I let myself roll out of the hammock into the long grass, pressing my face against the shiny glass bowl. When I was little, I used to think the bowl was like a crystal ball, that I could look into the glass, the water, and see a little glimpse of the future. I don't kid myself any more, and besides, there is no future in falling for a boy like Shay Fletcher, no future at all. The thing about a crush is that it's all one-sided. Shay probably just feels sorry for me, and even the novelty of that will wear off because I am only ever mean and horrible to him. Besides, he already has a girlfriend who is about a hundred times prettier than me.

As for sitting under the cherry trees with Shay Fletcher,

that was most definitely a bad, bad idea. He might think we are friends, but I am not so sure. Friendship isn't exactly what I feel when I think of Shay.

I don't think Honey would get it, either . . . if she knew about last night she would probably strangle me with her bare hands. And what would Skye, Summer and Coco say if they knew? Or Dad and Charlotte? I can't kid myself they would understand. Some things are just plain wrong, and hanging out after dark with your stepsister's boyfriend has got to be one of them.

I will walk down to the village and post my card to Mrs Mackie, then come back and do everything I can to make the things I have written come true.

There will be no more late-night stories, I promise myself. I have to stop this friendship now, before it messes everything up.

Rover stares at me, giving nothing away. That's the problem with telling your troubles to a goldfish. There is no chance of a cuddle or a discussion, no chance of a heart-to-heart. No matter how many times I ask him for advice, all I will get is the same cool, fishy gaze.

Typical.

'What are you doing?' a voice calls, and I sit up, brushing grass from my hair.

'Nothing!'

Coco flops down into the hammock beside me, and waves at Rover in his bowl. 'Do you talk to him?' she wants to know. 'Like people would with . . . well, a dog or something?'

'Of course not,' I lie. 'He's a fish! What would be the point?'

Coco shrugs. 'Fish have feelings too,' she says. 'Don't you ever feel sorry for him, swimming round in circles the whole time? I know you said you didn't want him to go in the duck pond, but we could make him a fish pond or something.'

I push the imagined Japanese-style pond out of my mind.

'Maybe,' I tell her. 'He doesn't need a pond, though. Fish have very short memories – three seconds, seriously. He's happy in his bowl.'

'Are you sure about the three seconds?' Coco frowns.

'I read it in a library book.'

'I'll check it on the Internet,' Coco decides. 'Only, if I was a fish, I'd like to have a proper pond. And other fish, as friends.'

'Rover is fine,' I say defensively. 'He doesn't need a whole bunch of fish to be happy.'

'OK,' Coco says. 'I was just saying . . .'

'He just needs me.'

'Sorr-ee.'

I pick up the bowl and carry it carefully across the grass to the caravan, and I set it back in place on top of the cupboard. Fish aren't like people, are they? They don't need fancy ponds or water lilies or stone pagodas. They don't need families, friends, dreams.

I peer at Rover. I was exactly like him, not so long ago . . . stuck in my own little goldfish-bowl world, swimming round and round in circles. Now everything has changed for me. My world has opened out, filled up with challenges and complications and possibilities. It's scary, sure, but I plan to give it my best shot. I am not going back to that little goldfish-bowl life, not if I can help it.

'Don't get any big ideas,' I tell Rover, and he gazes at me, faintly disapproving.

I think if Rover could talk, he would tell me not to get any big ideas either.

13

Summer has a ballet lesson in Minehead on Friday, and Charlotte takes Skye and me to do a supermarket shop while she's there. We drive past the high school I will be going to in September.

'It's a friendly place,' Charlotte says. 'And besides, Honey will look out for you.'

Skye looks at me and pulls a face.

'Er . . . right . . .' I mumble, but my heart sinks. Skye, Summer and Coco are still at middle school, of course. Just how will Honey look out for me, I wonder? By throwing my school books out of a top-floor window, my gym kit into a tree? That's something to look forward to.

Once Summer has finished her lesson, Charlotte takes

us down to the seafront so we can walk Fred along the sand, and she buys us all ice creams from a kiosk by the beach.

For a little while, eating ice cream with Charlotte, Summer and Skye, watching Fred ricochet across the sand, I forget about jigsaw pieces and misshapen Taystee Bars. I just relax and enjoy the sun on my face, the swish of cool water around my bare feet. Summer and Skye link my arms on either side and it feels good.

When we get back to Tanglewood, laden down with shopping, the kitchen looks like it has been burgled, vandalized and ransacked by a gang of maniacs. Dirty pans, dishes and trays are piled up in the sink, the dishwasher is chugging along full blast and Dad is scrubbing down the kitchen table. There is a strange, spicy aroma in the air, like chicken korma gone horribly wrong.

'Curry for tea?' Charlotte asks.

'Ah . . . no,' Dad admits. 'I've been experimenting with truffle flavours again. I've seen chilli chocolate out there, and I'm a big fan of Indian food –'

'Noooo,' I groan. 'Curry truffles? Seriously?'

'It may not be one of my better ideas,' Dad shrugs. 'Don't worry, though, I've tried a few other experiments as well . . . I've made six new flavours. I thought we could have a taste test, see which ones you all like!'

Charlotte looks around at the kitchen carnage, slightly shell-shocked.

'Lovely,' she says. 'Um . . . how often are you planning on making these chocolate experiments, Paddy? I'm not sure my nerves can take it.'

Dad looks crestfallen. 'I know the kitchen table isn't the best place for a chocolate business,' he admits. 'But I have some other ideas. Lots of ideas, actually. Now we've had a chance to settle in a bit, and everything is going so well, I thought perhaps we could make some plans? If we are really going to do this . . . well, we need to talk, get organized.'

Charlotte sinks down into an ancient armchair by the Aga.

'Sounds like time for a family meeting,' she sighs.

'Good idea!' Dad agrees. 'This will affect everyone. It's a family business.'

'Sounds serious,' Charlotte says.

'Very,' Dad agrees.

None of us has the heart to tell him he has chocolate smeared across his nose.

*

By the time Skye has tracked down Coco, Summer has unpacked the shopping and stacked it away, Dad and I have washed up the chocolate-caked pans and bowls, and the kitchen is looking a little less like the aftermath of a world war.

Charlotte pours cool fruit juices and Dad sets out plates of truffles along the centre of the table for us to taste. 'No sign of Honey?' Charlotte frowns. 'If this is a family meeting, she should be here too . . .'

'She was down at the beach,' Skye says. 'I told her to come up to the house, but she didn't seem too keen . . .'

Charlotte and Dad exchange a look. 'Well,' Dad says. 'Not to worry. We can always save some truffles for her to try later.'

The kitchen door swings open and Honey stalks in, wearing shorts and a T-shirt and heart-shaped sunglasses, as well as her usual scowl. 'What's all this rubbish?' she demands, glaring at the display of truffles. 'What's so important, anyway? I was busy – and anyhow, I don't eat chocolate! It gives you spots.'

She looks at me with a smirk, and I put a hand to my nose where a tiny Barbie-pink pimple has sprouted up overnight.

'Hey, c'mon, Honey, the truffles look good,' a second voice corrects her, and that's all I need. It's Shay, in cut-off jeans and a Muppets T-shirt, with the black beanie still slouching off the back of his head. My heart flips over at the sight of him.

He grins at me. 'Anyway, chocolate doesn't give you spots,' he says. 'It's just growing up that does that.'

'Growing up?' Honey says under her breath, shooting me a dark look. 'Yeah, right . . .'

I can feel my cheeks turning pinker than my spot. I get the message – there may only be a few months between me and Honey, age-wise, but it might as well be a lifetime. Honey looks grown-up, cool and sophisticated, and I look like a spotty little kid.

'Anyway, we're all here now,' Dad announces. 'So let's get started – I don't want to take up too much of your time. I've created some new truffle flavours for you to try, and I thought we could discuss a few other bits and pieces to do with the chocolate business –'

'What chocolate business?' Honey snarls, but Shay nudges her and she sighs and shuts up.

The tasting goes pretty well. Dad has made truffles

involving things like tiramisu and sherry trifle and fresh raspberries, and those all get the thumbs up. The ones involving curry and raw beetroot and parsley are not quite as successful, but that's not a big surprise to anyone but Dad.

'You have to push the boundaries,' he insists, wincing a little as he tries to swallow down one of the especially revolting beetroot truffles. 'Try new things. Find new tastes that nobody has discovered before . . .'

'Do people want to discover raw beetroot truffles?' Summer wonders out loud. 'Is the world ready for them?'

'I don't think so,' Skye muses, and Honey just rolls her eyes.

'Trust me,' Dad grins. 'I will discover something wonderful, one of these days. A taste that knocks your socks off, that makes us a fortune!'

'Well, you've got three amazing flavours there,' Charlotte says. 'That's a start.'

Honey picks up one of the beetroot truffles, looks at it disgustedly and chucks it in a perfect arc into the bin.

'They're just chocolates,' she argues. 'You can buy a hundred different brands of them, anywhere. And these aren't even proper chocolates, either! You're just melting down shop-bought stuff and turning it into something else. You're not going to make money out of something anyone can make themselves, at home. It's stupid!'

'Honey!' Shay says, but she just shrugs.

'Paddy knows what he's doing,' Charlotte says. 'Give this a chance, Honey. Hear him out!'

Dad looks round the table. 'Honey's right in a way,' he tells us. 'Making truffles on the kitchen table is not going to make anyone rich. We need to make our chocolate from scratch – source the best organic cocoa beans, roast them, crack and winnow them, grind them into a liqueur, conch and refine the chocolate and then temper it and create the final product. It's a complicated process. We'll need a gas grill, a roasting drum, a mill and a grinder –'

'How much is all that going to cost?' Honey cuts in. 'And where's the money going to come from? Not us, that's for sure. Mum, can't you see what all this is about? He thinks he can use your money to finance it all –'

'Honey!' Charlotte says. 'Stop that – right now! Paddy doesn't want my money, not that I have any to begin with. And this business is something we'd both like to do

. . . together. I won't have that kind of talk here, is that clear?'

Honey sets her face into a stony glare. Charlotte may turn a blind eye to most of her moods and strops, but it's clear she has her limits. She is not going to let Honey attack my dad.

Charlotte sighs, raking a hand through her blonde hair. 'My concern is where will we put all this stuff, Paddy? You're talking about specialist equipment. We'd need a decent space to work. We can't really spare the room without it damaging the B&B business, and as that's our bread and butter . . .'

'I know, I know,' Dad grins. 'Don't worry, I've got an idea. I've been looking at the old stable block behind the house. It's just full of junk at the moment, but I think I could convert it, turn it into a workshop or a small factory . . .'

'Willie Wonka eat your heart out,' Honey snorts. 'I don't think so. My dad used those stables to garage his old car, so stay away from it, Paddy Costello! You can't just barge in here and take over, building some ridiculous factory to make truffles nobody wants! Can nobody see how stupid this is?'

'Honey!' Charlotte says. 'That's enough! Apologize to Paddy right now!'

Honey gets to her feet, eyes blazing. 'Apologize?' she snarls. 'No way! I don't want you here . . . making your stupid curry truffles and your plans that won't ever get off the ground! You're not my dad!'

Dad raises his hands in a gesture of surrender. 'I know that –'

'You don't know anything!' Honey yells. 'You and Little Miss Perfect over there . . . dragging me up here to talk about your idiotic chocolates, calling a family meeting when you're not even family at all! And you never will be, OK? Not ever!'

Honey grabs the edges of the oilcloth tablecover and yanks it hard, pulling it off the table along with all the plates and glasses, the uneaten reject truffles. There is a sound of smashing crockery and glass, and Honey runs from the room in a blaze of blonde hair and fury, slamming the door behind her.

Dad sits down, resting his head in his hands.

'Oh dear,' he says.

14

'She'll calm down,' Shay says, settling himself in the armchair by the Aga while Dad tidies up the broken glass and china with a dustpan and brush, Fred at his heels, hoovering up the beetroot truffles. 'I'll go up and see her in a little while. Talk to her.'

He seems so calm, so laid back about it all. Somehow, that is infuriating.

'Shouldn't you go to her now?' I ask. 'She sounded pretty upset to me. And she is your girlfriend, right?'

'That's right,' Shay agrees. 'She is.'

I roll my eyes. 'So . . .?'

'So I think I'll let her calm down a little bit, first, before I try getting her to see sense,' he says with a shrug. 'No point in following her now and getting my head bitten off too . . .'

I say nothing, although the idea of Shay getting into a fight with Honey seems oddly satisfying. I realize I'm being mean – none of this is Shay's fault.

'I guess,' I sigh.

'Let's hope you can talk some reason into her, Shay,' Charlotte adds. 'You're so good with her . . . I never seem to say the right thing, these days. It's all so difficult! Are you staying for tea? It's just quiche and salad, but there's plenty of it . . .'

'Cool,' he grins.

Skye and Coco are setting the table for tea, spreading out a fresh checked cloth, arranging plates and cutlery, while Summer has a ballet CD in the player and is practising pliés with one hand on the dresser for balance.

Me, I just stand in the corner, carefully avoiding Shay's eyes, awkward, anxious. I am the one jigsaw puzzle piece that doesn't fit.

Shay picks up the blue guitar and strums a couple of chords, leaning back in the armchair like he is here to stay. He is so relaxed, so comfortable here, in a way I will never be. He just sat through a Tanberry family meeting and nobody batted an eyelid at his presence, even after what Honey said about Dad and me. It doesn't seem fair.

And I don't like the idea of him going up to talk to Honey, not one little bit.

'I didn't realize,' Dad is saying. 'About the stables. I didn't mean to upset Honey!'

'Everything seems to upset her, lately,' Charlotte tells him, slicing warm quiche. 'She's being unreasonable. Greg kept a car in those stables, sure – but that was then. He's not coming back, and Honey has to get used to that fact. Do whatever you want with the stable block, Paddy. We can't keep it as some kind of shrine to a car – or a relationship – that's long gone.

'Honey won't be happy whatever we do,' she goes on, shrugging as she rinses salad leaves. 'I'm sad about that, but what can I do? Honey has us all wound around her little finger, and I've let it happen . . . I've been scared to upset her. She takes everything so hard. First when Greg left, then when we got divorced, and this last year it's been because I've met someone new and fallen in love again . . . honestly, is that so wrong?'

'Of course not,' Dad tells her. 'Don't worry, love . . . she'll calm down.'

Charlotte sets potato salad, mixed leaves and two quiches on the table and we all sit down to eat, including Shay, who pours juice for everyone as if he is one of the family.

'So, what's this chocolate business going to be called?' he asks.

Dad blinks. 'Well . . . good question, Shay. We don't actually have a name yet. Any ideas? It has to be something strong, something different . . .'

'You could name it after me,' Coco says. 'Cool Coco.'

'Good one,' Dad grins. 'Appropriate too! But what about Skye and Summer and Honey and Cherry? Charlotte too! I'd have to give you all a mention!'

I am not convinced that being name-checked in the chocolate business would please Honey, but I let this pass.

'How about Kitnor Chocolates?' Summer offers. 'Simple and direct.'

'Tanglewood Truffles?' Skye suggests.

'Good,' Dad agrees. 'We need something memorable,

something strong. It doesn't have to be local, though, because we have big ideas for this business!'

'What kind of image are you trying to create?' Shay asks. 'Luxury chocolates? Handmade? Organic, fairly traded? You need an image, a gimmick.'

'The gimmick could be unexpected tastes,' Summer suggests. 'Beetroot bonbons. Chocolate curry. You could call it Traumatic Truffles . . .'

'Sickening Sweets?' Coco grins.

'Maybe not,' Dad laughs. 'I think I'll stick with the edible ones . . .'

'I liked it when you used to send little boxes of them through the post,' Skye chips in. 'That was cool.'

'Oh, that was fun to do,' I tell her. 'We used to get card and decorate it with paint and patterns and little messages, then Dad would draw on a template for a box and score along the folds and we'd have this perfect, tiny box for the truffles.'

'And you lined them with gold tissue paper and tied them up with ribbon,' Charlotte remembers. 'They were really special . . . I still have some of the boxes. That would make our product different, Paddy – beautiful little boxes with handpainted designs, tied up with ribbon . . .'

Dad's eyes light up. 'You're right – we need a unique look, something different from the things already available in the shops. That could be it! A real artisan product, luxurious and stylish . . . that's the message we want!'

'Are you going to sell from shops, or do mail order?' Shay wants to know. 'I can just imagine getting a parcel through the post, and inside there's this really cool little box . . .'

'. . . full of beetroot and curry truffles,' Skye teases.

'Full of beautiful, handcrafted chocolates,' Dad corrects her. 'We could get shops to stock us, and sell by mail order too . . . get a website. Either way, we want to stand out from the crowd, be different, special. And if the chocolates themselves are a little bit different, then the packaging needs to be too . . .'

An idea pops into my head, and I just about choke on a mouthful of quiche. 'That's what you can call the business,' I say. 'The Chocolate Box!'

'The Chocolate Box?' Dad echoes. 'I like that.'

'It's good – simple,' Charlotte agrees.

'Easy to remember,' Skye adds.

Shay grins, and for a moment, his sea-green eyes meet mine. 'Perfect,' he says.

By the time we've polished off the quiche and salad, a plan has taken shape.

The business will be called The Chocolate Box, and Charlotte will start working on a website for it straight away, because she knows about that kind of stuff and runs her own website for the B&B. Dad will start converting the stables and will see the bank next week to talk about getting a loan for the machinery and raw materials. He will order in some gold tissue paper and ribbon and sheets of stiff card in red, pink and black so we can paint them with gold and silver and rainbow paint, adding hearts and stars and little handwritten messages among the patterns.

'I know we're not ready to make chocolates from scratch just yet,' Charlotte says. 'But there's a Food Festival in Kitnor every August, and we'd be crazy not to take advantage of that. It could get us some useful publicity.'

'Sounds good,' Dad agrees. 'How do we get involved?'

'They do a Food Trail,' Charlotte explains. 'It's like a map of the area, with all the food businesses marked on it. We could sign up for it . . . we should just about have time. On that particular day, the whole village is buzzing with tourists, moving from one place to the next, looking at how things are made, buying all this special, carefully crafted food. If we're a part of that . . . well, it'd be the best way I can think of to launch the business!'

Dad's eyes are shining. 'We'll do it,' he says. 'The timing will be tight, but you're right, Charlotte, it's a chance we can't afford to miss.'

'Sounds like a plan,' I grin.

We're all smiling, clearing up empty plates and collecting up glasses, when an ear-splitting thud of bass starts up above us. It might have been music, once, but it is turned up so loud it is hard to be sure. Right now, it's more of an assault, an attack, a thumping headache of around a million decibels that shudders through the house and makes the ceiling quiver.

'What the –?' Dad asks, clapping his hands over his ears.

'It's Honey,' Charlotte sighs. 'Oh, lord, she's going to deafen the guests, or blow the roof off, or both . . . I really don't think my nerves can take this!'

'She's probably hacked off that I haven't put in an appearance yet,' Shay says, guiltily, grabbing up his blue guitar. 'Don't worry. I'll sort it.'

A minute later the racket is cut off abruptly, and every-

✿✿✿✿✿✿✿✿✿✿✿✿✿✿✿✿✿✿✿✿✿✿✿✿✿✿✿

one breathes a sigh of relief. Another disaster has been averted, for now at least.

Like Rapunzel in the tower, Honey has reeled in her prince, cast her spell . . . and Shay is lost.

15

After the chocolate discussion and the noise war and Shay's hasty exit, the rest of us head for the squashy sofas in the living room and Charlotte puts on a DVD of a film called *Chocolat*. 'You'll like it,' she tells me. 'Trust me . . . just grab yourself a bit of sofa and settle in . . .'

The sofas are huge, like soft velvet islands arranged round a shaggy cream-coloured rug. When you sit down you just sink into them, like you're sitting on a cloud. They are a long way from the sagging brown corduroy sofa back in Glasgow. Dad and Charlotte snuggle up together on one, me, Skye and Summer on the other. Coco stretches out on the rug, with Fred beside her.

Shoes are not allowed, of course, but we put our feet up and curl up, and as the film wears on Skye slumps back until she is leaning against her twin, her legs stretched out in my lap. We are a jumble of limbs, a lazy, comfortable, sisterly heap. It makes me smile.

As for the DVD, it's awesome. It's about a mysterious mother and daughter who turn up unexpectedly in this crazy French village and start turning everything upside down with their little chocolate shop. There are river gypsies and chocolate festivals and friendship and feuds and magic, and it makes me believe that we can have a chocolate business, and that it will be a very, very long way from the misshapen Taystee Bars.

'We could have a chocolate festival too,' I say. 'For that Food Trail day.'

Charlotte raises an eyebrow. 'We could,' she agrees. 'We really could. It's a very, very good idea!'

'Genius,' Dad blinks.

'The garden would be perfect for it,' Summer says. 'We could have stalls and games and chocolate-tasting and chocolate-themed entertainment . . .'

'We can all help,' Coco offers.

'Spread the word!' says Skye. 'And weave a little magic.'

Sounds good to me.

*

I walk down to the caravan later, Fred at my side. I breathe in the darkness, the cool air folding itself around me like a promise. Silence drips from the treetops like rain, and the fairy lights twinkle and glint, and Fred runs ahead, chasing imaginary rabbits, sniffing through the undergrowth.

I can see the caravan, a dark, curving silhouette beneath the trees, and then a soft guitar chord breaks the silence and Fred starts barking and I just about jump out of my skin.

A blond-fringed boy is sitting on the caravan steps, grinning.

'Shay!' I yelp. 'What are you doing? Ambushing me and scaring me half to death . . .'

Shay Fletcher is easily the most confusing boy I have ever met. When I am with him, my emotions are all over the place . . . irritation, anger, jealousy . . . and a whole bunch of other things I daren't even admit to.

'How am I ambushing you?' he asks. 'I was just taking a rest on my way home . . .'

'Yeah, right.'

He looks guilty. 'Well, OK, I was waiting for you, but that's not an ambush, is it? I wanted to talk.'

'Good plan,' I say. 'We chat away while your plate-smashing, ear-mangling girlfriend trashes the house and plots how best to strangle me with her bare hands . . .'

'Huh?'

'Oh, never mind,' I sigh. 'Look, you shouldn't be here.'

'Where should I be?' Shay asks.

'Somewhere else,' I say. 'Anywhere else.'

He grins. 'I'm flexible. We could go to the beach, if you like. Paddle in the ocean, watch the stars. But we had a deal, you were telling me your story, I was playing you my songs –'

'It wasn't a deal!'

'It was,' Shay insists. 'A deal between friends.'

I bite my lip. I know the rules, and Shay is out of bounds. Every teen mag I have ever read is very clear about that. It's just that I'm finding it hard to remember why the rules are so strict, after what Honey has said to Dad and me. She is mean and sour and spiteful, and she wants us out of here.

Even after hours of chilling out with Dad, Charlotte, Skye, Summer and Coco, Honey's words still sting. I don't think that anything I do could please her . . . and suddenly, I am tired of trying so hard.

If I were friends with Shay . . . just friends . . . would that be so wrong?

'Maybe,' I hear myself say, and Shay's eyes shine.

'Great, I want us to be friends. I like you, Cherry, I really do . . . you listen to me.'

'So what did you want to talk about?' I ask.

Shay sighs. 'Trust me, you don't want to know. My dad hates me, my girlfriend is turning into a psycho and I'm supposed to sit back and soak it all up. Nobody ever thinks I might be having a hard time. Well, except for you. And even you can't work out if you like me or hate me, most of the time.'

'I like you, Shay,' I admit. 'It's just . . . complicated.'

'Tell me about it,' he huffs. 'But really . . . you're different. Interesting.'

'I'm not that interesting,' I say.

'I think you are . . .'

My heart starts doing triple somersaults, at just about the same time as my head starts telling me to run for the hills. I want to be interesting. It may not be quite as enticing as gorgeous or sexy or whatever he thinks that Honey is, but it's something. Interesting . . . that is something I have always wanted to be, and somehow never was.

'Anyhow . . . it's a long story, and I don't think it's going to have a happy ending.' Shay leans back against the caravan door, sighing. 'My life sucks, seriously. Tell me about Sakura instead . . . please?'

I sit down on the fallen tree trunk, Fred loafing at my feet. Shay is right – sometimes, stories are better than reality. And much more interesting, of course, particularly if you're me.

I take a deep breath and tell Shay the story of the kimono and the fan.

'There was a very special festival in Kyoto,' I begin. 'Maybe five or six months before the day in the park when Sakura saw the cherry blossoms fall. On the day of this festival, parents who had children aged seven, five or three years old would take them to the shrine to give thanks for their health and pray for future blessings. Sakura was three, so her parents hired a tiny silk kimono to dress her in, and put a clip trimmed with cherry blossom in her hair.'

Shay smiles in the darkness.

'Sakura's dad wore a black kimono, and her mum wore one made of heavy salmon-pink silk with a deep orange lining, handpainted with cherry blossom and flying birds, all shot through with gold thread.

'At the shrine, Sakura was allowed to pull on the bell rope and clap three times to summon the gods, and her mum wrote a prayer on to a little wooden board to hang up to bring good luck. Back home, she was given a present, a paper fan painted with cherry blossom. It was a perfect day, and Sakura knew she would remember it forever . . .'

'Wow,' Shay says. 'I can't imagine you at three years old, living on a whole different continent . . .'

'Shhh,' I tell him. 'The story isn't finished. I've already told you about the day Sakura saw the cherry blossom fall, and then, later, how she woke up one day and found her mother gone . . . that was maybe a year after the festival. Sakura didn't understand. She missed her mum, and often asked about her, wanting to know where she had gone, and why, and when she might be coming home.

'Sakura's dad was silent and sad, and he never answered her questions but just lifted her up and hugged her close.

Sometimes Sakura would feel his eyelashes, damp with tears, brushing against her cheek. She knew that he missed Kiko just as much as she did . . .' I stop talking then.

Shay gets up from the caravan steps and walks over to sit beside me. I flinch away from him, but Shay slides an arm round me and I am lost. I want nothing more than to curl up against him, press my cheek against his shoulder.

I don't, of course. Fred, the best guard dog in the whole universe, rescues me by pushing between us, resting his head on my knee. 'Hey, hey, Fred,' I laugh, running my fingers through his bird's-nest fur. I pull away from Shay again, and this time he lets me go, takes up his guitar and picks out a few sad chords.

'Anyway,' I continue. 'A few months later, Sakura's dad gave her a package wrapped in rustling tissue paper, and when she unwrapped it she discovered the salmon-pink kimono her mum had worn on the day of the festival. Sakura lifted up the heavy silk, traced her fingers over the handpainted birds and the cherry blossom. She pressed her face against the fabric and breathed in jasmine and powder, the soft, sweet smell of her mum, and for the first time since Kiko had gone, Sakura began to cry.'

Shay sighs and puts his guitar down on the grass.

'Whoa,' he whispers. 'That was the kimono that Honey threw out of the window?'

'Charlotte washed it,' I say in a small voice. 'She was trying to make it fresh and new again, but now it just smells of washing powder . . . there's nothing left of my mum.'

Shay squeezes my hand in the darkness. 'There's a lot of her left, I bet,' he whispers. 'She's in you.'

Shay stands up, pulling down a tree branch to pick a handful of cherries. He leans towards me in the darkness, draping a little cherry bunch over each of my ears, like outsize, dangly earrings, and I shiver, even though the night is warm.

Then he slings the blue guitar over one shoulder and walks away, leaving me with a racing heart and a head full of dreams that have nothing to do with friendship, nothing at all.

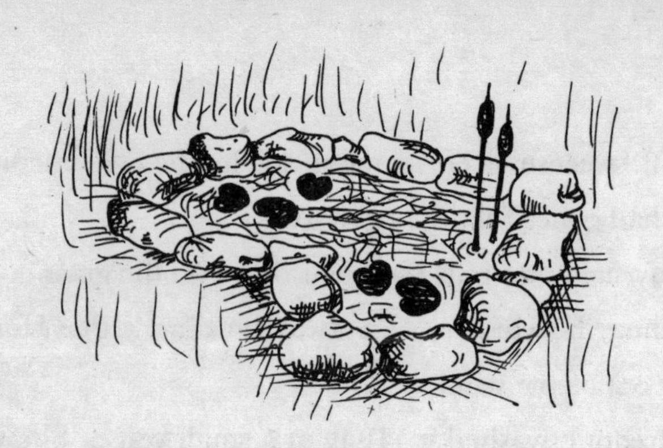

16

I wake up in a tangle of sheets, Fred snuggled into me, sunlight sneaking through the caravan curtains. And then I remember last night, and guilt aches in my throat like a sickness.

Why did I let Shay stick around? I promised myself I was going to stop, then caved in almost at once. I sigh. When Shay is around, my determination crumbles into dust.

As I wander up to the house in bare feet and PJs, I hear the strains of Dad's favourite fiddle CD drifting down towards me, punctuated with sudden loud crashes and bangs. I follow the sound and discover Dad, in ancient jeans and a cobwebby T-shirt, dragging boxes, bin bags and broken bits of furniture out of the old stable block while a little CD player sits on the tack room window sill, spilling out upbeat folky sounds.

'Morning, Cherry!' Dad grins. 'Thought I'd make a start! Got enough stuff here for a dozen bonfires, and there'll be a good few trips to the tip as well . . .'

'Great,' I say weakly. 'I'll help if you want . . . I slept in, and I haven't got any plans . . .'

'No, no, you go and hang out with the girls,' Dad insists. 'I'm enjoying it!'

He heads back inside and a moment later a couple of dusty, down-at-heel kitchen chairs fly out and land on the mounting pile of junk.

I sigh and head inside to shower and dress. I fix myself some toast and help Charlotte stack the dishwasher and tidy the kitchen after the breakfast rush. Skye has gone down to the village to see a friend and Summer has a dance class in town, so Coco and I help Charlotte to clean the guest bedrooms and then I head back to the caravan to read for a while.

'How's your fish getting on?' Coco asks, tagging along.

'Rover is fine,' I say. 'Better than fine.'

'It's just that I've been investigating,' she shrugs. 'The

latest research on goldfish suggests that they have much better memories than anyone thought. Seriously. Like, five or six seconds instead of three. At least. Rover could feel really lonely, swimming around in that bowl for years and years with only a luminous pink bridge and a bit of plastic weed to liven things up.'

I pick up my book and frown at Rover. 'Six seconds,' I sigh. 'It's still a very short space of time.'

'I know, but . . . well, you want the best for him, don't you?'

'Who are you, Doctor Dolittle?' I say. 'Rover is my pet. I look after him well. He loves me!'

'I know that,' Coco says. 'And you love him. But just think, if he had a pond of his own . . .'

I take a long, hard look at Rover, and remember the pond I imagined for him, with water lilies and a stone pagoda and a bridge. It would be fish-heaven.

I love having him in the caravan with me, but maybe he deserves more than that?

'Do you really think he'd like it?' I ask.

'Trust me,' Coco grins. 'He'd love it. A goldfish in a bowl lives maybe five, ten years . . . if he is lucky. And of course, he'd never grow big, because there's no room to grow.'

'Rover's quite big,' I say. 'But if he was in a pond, he'd seem really, really tiny. He might be out of his depth.'

Coco laughs. 'Right now, Rover is a little fish in a teeny-tiny pond,' she says. 'A goldfish-bowl, in fact. There is nothing left for him to explore, nothing left for him to learn. Take a risk. Let him be a little fish in a big pond! Trust me, fish don't mind being out of their depth. They like it!'

'I suppose . . .'

I think about how I felt, when I first arrived at Tanglewood House. I was out of my depth too, but there was a buzz of excitement, of possibility, as well. It was the start of something new, and I liked that feeling.

Maybe Rover would too?

'He'll grow,' Coco says. 'And he'll probably live longer. He'll be happy.'

That swings it, really.

'It can't be all that hard to dig a fish pond,' Coco says. 'I'll look it up on the Internet. We can put it by the patio, so the guests can see it.'

'Might be cool,' I say. 'OK, let's do it!'

Coco grins. 'I'll ask Charlotte,' she says.

The next day, we are in the middle of breakfast when there's a knock on the kitchen door. A bloke in blue overalls is there, grinning. 'You wanted a digger?' he says.

'A digger?' Charlotte echoes, frying pan in hand. 'No, no, we didn't want a digger, Joe. Where did you get that idea?'

'Young Coco rang up last night,' he says. 'Something about a fish pond?'

Charlotte looks at Coco, who is trying hard to hide behind a Cornflakes box. 'We hadn't agreed on a pond, Coco,' she says mildly. 'I just said I'd think about it.'

'You said it was a very good idea,' Coco reminds her. 'In principle. And now that the digger's here . . . it'd be a shame not to use it, right?'

'But where would we put a fish pond?' Charlotte asks.

'Up near the house, by the patio,' Coco says.

Dad nods. 'We could do. The guests might like it. It could be a feature.'

'But it's such a lot of work.' Charlotte frowns. 'You're

clearing out the stables, and there's the festival to prepare for, and both of us are supposed to be working on our presentation for the bank to try to get a loan for The Chocolate Box!'

Dad shrugs. 'Do you really want a pond?'

'Yes!' I say. 'It's for Rover! So he feels like he really belongs.'

'Well, I'm nipping into town later anyway,' Dad says. 'I have to go to the tip and hire a pressure washer to clean down the walls and floor in the stable. If I'm in the DIY store I can get a pond liner, and the girls could do the rest. Right, Coco, Cherry?'

'Right!' we chorus.

'We'll help,' Skye chips in.

'Sure, it'd be fun,' Summer agrees.

'So,' asks the bloke in the doorway, 'do you want this digger or not?'

By the time Charlotte has served eggs Benedict to table six and kippers on toast to table three, Joe the digger man has gouged a huge hole next to the patio. A mound of soil the size of the red minivan is piled up beside it, and the digger is trundling off along the gravel drive.

'Oh dear,' Coco says. 'That's a LOT of soil.'

We drive into Minehead, ditch a trailerful of soil and junk at the tip and head on to the DIY superstore to buy acres of thick black pond-liner, three water lilies in under-water buckets, six sacks of gravel and some barrel tubs to fill with soil and plant up with bedding plants.

There are also four new goldfish from the pet shop to keep Rover company. We took ages, picking out fish that looked different from Rover, so we could tell them all apart. One has a very fancy tail, one has a black patch on his side, one has a notched fin, one has silvery-white blotches on gold.

'What should we call them?' Coco wonders. 'Goldie and Lola and Silvertail and Princess?'

'Or Fido and Patch and Spot and Butch,' I suggest. 'So that Rover feels at home.'

Dad nods his approval. He spends the morning helping us to make the pond, arranging rocks and gravel round the edge to hide the liner. Dad heads back to the workshop in the afternoon, and we start filling the pond with water. By teatime it is almost ready. We lower the water lilies into position and shovel the mountain of soil into the barrel containers, stuff in the bedding plants and arrange them on the patio. We are just brushing away the last of the soil when Charlotte comes out with lemonade on a tray, a reward for the workers.

'It looks very nice,' she admits. 'You've all worked really hard!'

There is no stone pagoda, no Japanese footbridge, but there could be . . . one day. Charlotte is right, the pond is cool. Any fish would be proud to have a home like that.

Dad says we have to wait a day to let the water warm and settle before the fish move in, and I am secretly glad to have one more night alone with Rover, just like old times.

'Everything's changing,' I tell him, huddled in my bunk in the caravan. 'For both of us. It's time to move on, grow up. We are part of a proper family now.'

Rover blinks.

'You mustn't think that it's too big or too posh for you,' I tell him. 'You deserve it, after all this time in a little glass bowl. And don't worry about the other fish. You'll get used to them. I got used to Tanglewood House, didn't I? And Charlotte and Skye and Summer and Coco. I might even get used to Honey, in the end.'

I count to six, watching him carefully. 'Are you listening?' I ask. 'You need to remember this, and remember it for more than six seconds. It's important.'

Rover flicks his tail.

'I will still come and see you every day,' I promise him. 'I will still feed you. You will grow, and learn, and have adventures. You will live to be very old, and very wise. One day, you might even be a big fish in a small pond! And I will still love you more than any of the other goldfish, I promise.'

I blow a kiss against the cool glass, and snuggle down beneath the covers to sleep.

17

A few days later I am lying flat out on the grass beside the new pond, staring down into the water, when a pair of blue strappy sandals step into the edge of my vision.

'Don't do it,' a cool, bored voice says. 'Don't jump.'

I scramble to a sitting position. Honey is looking down at me, an expression of pity in her eyes.

'I was just looking for my fish,' I say, as if this is somehow normal behaviour. 'Rover.'

Honey perches on one of the patio benches. 'Don't you think it's weird?' she says. 'Calling your goldfish a dog's name?'

'Someone else said that, once,' I sigh, thinking of Kirsty McRae. 'You remind me of her, funnily enough.'

Honey raises an eyebrow and twists her mouth into an especially Kirsty-like scowl.

'I think it's funny,' I shrug. 'About the name. Ironic, y'know?'

'Right,' she says, unimpressed. 'Why were you looking for your goldfish anyhow? Don't tell me, you talk to him, tell him all your secrets.'

'Of course I don't,' I bluff. 'That would be crazy.'

Rover glides soundlessly to the surface. I'd almost swear he's laughing. He flicks his tail and dives down beneath the water lilies again, a small fish in a big pond, enjoying every minute.

Honey opens up a sketchbook and takes a pencil from behind her ear, frowning thoughtfully. 'I have stuff to do for my art project,' she says. 'And you happen to be in the way.'

She smiles sweetly, her waist-length blonde hair fanned out around her like a golden cloak. I think she just told me to push off out of her sight, but I can't quite believe it.

'Honey, I know you don't much like me being here . . .'

'Much?' she echoes, smirking.

I sigh. 'OK then, you don't like me being here at all. But

I am here, and so is Dad, so don't you think it would be better if we all tried to get along?'

'Are you stupid?' Honey sighs. 'Don't you understand? I know the others are humouring you, but seriously, you must realize this whole stepfamily thing is not going to work. You will never fit in here, Cherry, no matter how hard you try.'

My cheeks flush pink and I feel like I've been slapped.

Fitting in . . . how can she tell that is the thing I want most of all? To belong, to be a part of things? I thought I was doing OK, but Honey's words crush my hopes like eggshells.

'There is no point in us trying to get on, Cherry,' she goes on. 'Face it – I can't stand you. And you probably can't stand me. End of story.'

I am not too keen on Honey Tanberry, it's true, but it is very hard to like someone who clearly cannot stand you. Honey looks at me like I am an especially repellent slug that has crawled up on to her suede strappy sandals.

Beneath the pretty princess exterior, Honey is kind of poisonous . . . but still, there is a part of me that longs for her to accept me, like me.

Like that is ever going to happen.

'It's not really about us, though, is it?' I argue. 'Honey,

don't you think your mum and my dad deserve a chance to be happy?'

Her blue eyes flash with fury. 'Oh, don't pretend you care about that!' she snaps. 'As if! You march in here and act like you own the place . . . you must think you've really hit it lucky, but it won't last, trust me. Your dad is a clown. He couldn't get this chocolate business off the ground if his life depended on it, and when he fails, Mum will chuck him out. She doesn't like wasters.'

I swallow back my own anger. 'You're wrong about Dad,' I tell her. 'He's . . . he's great, and Charlotte likes him, I know she does.'

'For now,' Honey shrugs. 'She liked my dad too, and then she changed her mind and threw him out. So don't go getting too comfortable, OK? Your days are numbered. I write to Dad all the time, so he knows exactly what's going on, and trust me, he is not impressed. He still loves Mum – this split, it's just a blip . . .'

Honey smiles, a soft, sweet smile that almost has me believing her. I can see a couple of the new goldfish, gliding around beneath the surface, almost unseen, and I wonder what's going on beneath the surface with Honey.

Nothing good, I suspect.

'But . . . the split was three years ago. They're divorced, aren't they? I mean, it's all final and everything . . .'

Honey rolls her eyes. 'The divorce was a mistake. Dad was just angry with Mum . . . he loves us, all of us. We're going to be a family again.'

I have a feeling that most of this is wishful thinking – if Greg Tanberry was planning a big family reunion, wouldn't he be sending flowers and calling round and trying to put things right? From what I have heard, he is holed up in a luxury London flat and hasn't been near Kitnor since the day he was thrown out.

'I don't think Charlotte wants that,' I say gently.

Honey curls her lip. 'You'd be surprised. Paddy is so not her type, trust me. My dad is a proper businessman, with Armani suits and sports cars and a gold watch . . . your dad worked in a chocolate factory! And don't even think about telling me that rubbish about him being a manager, because I asked him myself and he said his job was picking out the reject chocolate bars. I don't think you need to be a manager to do that!'

My cheeks burn, and I look away.

'Trust me,' Honey goes on. 'My dad is the real deal. He makes Paddy look like a . . . a gypsy!'

I think of Mrs Mackie's song about the raggle-taggle gypsies and the DVD we watched the other day, *Chocolat*, and I think that sometimes a man who looks like a gypsy may be exactly what you might dream of. I have seen Charlotte look at Dad, and I think that she loves him almost as much as I do . . . it's one of the reasons I think she's so cool.

'My dad is a high-flyer,' Honey ploughs on. 'He works really hard. All hours, seven days a week. That's why I can't just phone him whenever I like, because he could be in the middle of some big business meeting. That's why he can't always come down here and see us, and why he sometimes has to cancel if we're going up to London to see him . . .'

I bite my lip. If Honey is trying show me how much better her dad is than mine, it's not working. All I can see is a flashy, shallow bloke who puts work ahead of his daughters, but Honey sees it all through rose-coloured glasses. She loves her dad, though, and that's something I do know about.

'Look, Honey,' I say carefully, 'I know you don't think much of me, but we do have one thing in common. You've lost someone you love, and that happened to me too, with my mum . . . it hurts. It hurts a lot.'

Honey rolls her eyes. 'I haven't lost my dad,' she says scathingly. 'What does that even mean? You make it sound like I've mislaid him, like I've been careless somehow and forgotten where he is! I know where my dad is and trust me, he isn't lost. It's a totally different situation.'

There's a stab of pain inside my chest and I tilt my chin up defiantly, determined not to show it. Honey knows about my mum – she must do – but she doesn't care. I will never find any common ground with her, that much is clear. If the two of us were shipwrecked on a desert island, she'd probably jump into the ocean and start swimming, just to get away from me.

I get up off the grass, head held high, cheeks burning. Every part of me is trembling with hurt and anger, but I can't let Honey see that . . . I won't.

'Cherry?'

I meet her eyes, waiting for the next attack, but it doesn't come.

'I am sorry about your mum,' she says quietly. 'I'm not a total bitch, you know.'

My eyes open wide and I can't think of anything to say, anything at all. Did I just find a chink in Honey's armour? Maybe she has a heart, after all . . . and maybe there is hope for us yet.

Or maybe not.

'This isn't personal, OK?' she says. 'I just want to make sure you know. For everyone's sake. The truth is, my mum's just using Paddy to make Dad jealous. So . . . now you know. And there's really no point in us trying to get along, Cherry, because you probably won't even be here by this time next week. OK?'

I turn and walk away.

18

I haven't seen Shay for a week – not properly, not alone. That's a good thing, I know, even though it doesn't feel that way.

The first few nights I lie awake at night, waiting for a knock on the caravan door that never comes. After another few days of no-show, I tell myself I'm glad. I stop expecting him, stop hoping, decide it's for the best because the two of us have no future anyhow. This is the way it has to be.

When I do see Shay, though, calling for Honey to take her to some get-together, or lazing in the hammock in the warm summer evenings or inviting himself for tea yet again, it's like a twist of the knife. My stomach churns and my heart races and I have to look away before the whole world catches on that I am crushing on my stepsister's boyfriend.

I think of Honey, sitting on the window seat in her turret room, the thick rope of plait hanging over her shoulder, waiting. I always imagined she was waiting for her prince, for Shay, but now I think that she's waiting for someone else entirely, someone smooth and slick and always out of reach.

She's waiting for a dad who will never come home. She's living in a fantasy world, and that is something I know all about . . . after all, I've done it myself for long enough. I lived so much in a world of dreams and lies that I forgot to pay much attention to the present, but now, for the first time ever, I have a present that's worth living in, worth fighting for.

I am not about to put all that in danger just because I have fallen for a boy who belongs to someone else.

I have done a lot of thinking, and no matter how I add it all up, the answers come out the same. Crushing on a boy who has a girlfriend is bad news, and when that girlfriend happens to be your new stepsister you are looking at the kind of scenario that could easily spark off World

War Three. I can't stand the guilt and I can't stand the waiting and I seriously cannot stand the longing, the dreaming, for a boy who is way out of bounds.

It's time to take control.

I have made a decision. I will not be telling stories in the dark any more, weaving pictures around my past, bringing memories back to life while a blond-fringed boy listens and strums his blue guitar. In fact, there will be no more stories, full stop. It is not a good plan.

Shay Fletcher and me, we're over. Not that we ever really started, of course.

When Shay comes calling round to the caravan, a few nights later, I am ready.

He knocks on the door, raps on the glass of the little window. 'Cherry?' he whispers. 'It's me! Are you awake?'

Fred whines and whimpers and tries to run over to the door, but I hold his collar tightly and pull the quilt over my head. I lie silent and still, until the knocking stops and I hear the sound of footsteps moving away through the grass, and then I cry myself to sleep.

The next morning, I am coming out of the caravan when

I see a small, torn square of creamy paper speared on to a branch of the cherry tree above my head. I stretch up and take down the little square of paper, smooth it out.

Written across it in blotchy black pen are three lines of scruffy, spidery writing:

A silk kimono
Flutters in the treetops
Scent of jasmine and tears

My heart flips over and my cheeks flame. Shay Fletcher.

I sink down on to the caravan steps. Do friends leave each other Japanese haiku, hanging on trees in the middle of the night? I don't think so. Guilt and hope curl together inside me, replaced by determination.

How come doing the right thing sometimes feels so wrong?

Does Shay Fletcher vanish from my life? I wish.

Suddenly he is everywhere . . . watching DVDs in the evening, curled up on the blue velvet sofas, making himself late-night cheese sandwiches in the kitchen, lounging in the hammock with his blue guitar.

'Where were you?' he asks quietly, the first time we cross paths. 'I called for you the other night, but I don't think you were there . . .'

I can't meet his eyes. 'I was there,' I tell him.

'I guess you were sleeping,' he says hopefully. 'I should have knocked louder.'

'I wasn't sleeping,' I whisper. 'I just thought . . . well, it's not such a good idea, is it? Us being friends. And besides . . . do friends write poetry for each other?'

Shay exhales, blowing upwards at the blond fringe. 'What poetry?' he bluffs.

'Come on, Shay. I know it was you. It had to be you.'

'Didn't you like it?' he asks.

'I didn't say I didn't like it!' I argue. 'I do like it . . . I'm just saying. Us being friends . . . it's not gonna work.'

'No?'

'No. Stay away . . . I mean it, Shay.'

I expect him to argue, to challenge me, try to talk me round, but he doesn't. He just smiles at me sadly, his eyes accusing, as if I've done something awful, like set fire to his black beanie hat or flicked chewing gum into his fringe.

Luckily, where Shay is, Honey is never far behind. She glides up silently, shark-like.

'Come on,' she says to Shay. 'We've got things to do . . .' She hooks an arm through his and tows him away.

There is no escape, though – or not for long.

Even in the daytime, when Shay is meant to be safely out of the way, working at his holiday job at the sailing centre, he still manages to appear. I am down at the beach with the twins, yelping and shrieking and splashing around in the waves with Skye, when out of nowhere, Shay drifts past in a canoe with a flotilla of tourists in orange life jackets bobbing along behind him.

'Hey!' he yells and lifts an oar in greeting, splashing us with silvery spray. I can't help noticing that he is still wearing his black beanie hat, even though the sun is beating down. I cannot see the blue guitar, but it's quite possible he has it stashed away inside the canoe.

I duck under the water until he and his crew have splashed on out of sight round the bay, then retreat to the safety of the sand, where Summer is stretched out reading a ballet book.

'That boy is everywhere,' I tell her crossly. 'It's like he haunts this place. Hasn't he got a home of his own?'

'Shay does spend a lot of time at Tanglewood,' she admits. 'When he's not working, that is. Mum sometimes jokes that we've adopted him.'

'That's all I need,' I huff.

'His charm doesn't work on you, does it?' she says, and I sigh because of course Shay's charm works much too well on me and there is no way on earth I can let that show.

'Weird,' Summer says. 'Girls are usually all over Shay Fletcher like a rash. All my friends are crushing on him. He's kind and friendly and sort of flirty. I mean, I don't feel that way about him. Obviously . . . he's just Honey's boyfriend . . . but I do like him. He has this way of talking to you like you're the only one in the room. Know what I mean?'

'No,' I bluff. 'Not really. And why does he have to lead his canoe expeditions right past here? This bay is meant to be private!'

Skye wades out of the water, wrapping herself in a towel, and pads across to join us.

'I wish!' Summer is saying. 'The beach is public property, Cherry. Anyone can walk past, or swim or sunbathe or picnic. And Shay is taking grockles round to the smugglers' caves, it's a part of his job . . . all the tourists want to see them.'

'The caves are our local tourist attraction,' Skye agrees, flopping down on to the sand. 'You can't actually drive there or even walk there very easily . . . they're cut off by rocks and cliffs on both sides, so there's this perfect bay that is only properly accessible by boat. The smugglers landed their contraband and hid it in the caves, and the customs and excise men could never find them. No wonder this area did so well with smuggling in the past!'

'What did they smuggle, exactly?'

'Everything, pretty much,' Skye shrugs. 'Brandy and gin and silk and cotton and coffee and tea . . . there used to be really big taxes for importing stuff in those days, and the smugglers were bringing things in without having to pay the taxes. All the locals were in on it. They cut this really steep, secret pathway up the hillside, through the woods, to get the stuff out . . . they'd keep what they wanted and take the rest up to the towns and cities to make a profit. It was big business.'

I lie back on the warm sand and close my eyes, trying to imagine smugglers in stripy sailor tops rolling barrels of brandy across the beach and hiding out in dark, damp caves. But in my dream, the smuggler turns round and he's wearing a black beanie hat and carrying a blue guitar, and I know then that there is no escape for me, and no hope, not ever.

19

If you want to forget someone, you have to stay busy, that's what the teen mags say. You have to work, as hard as you possibly can, to keep your mind off your crush. And a crush, of course, is all that this is. It's not like it is anything more, anything real, anything serious.

A crush, according to the teen mags, is a one-way love affair. The boy you are crushing on invades your dreams, your head, your heart. You think about him first thing in the morning and last thing at night, and you imagine a million different ways you can be together, but it's all for nothing, because he is out of reach. Usually, that means he is a movie star or a rock god or some local heart-throb who doesn't even know you are alive, but of course, things are more complicated for me.

So I am staying busy, and hoping that the crush will fade. I am doing my best to do the right thing, even though I secretly want to do the wrong thing.

I am trying.

Dad is making progress with the old stable block, running pipes along from the main water supply and hiring a cement mixer to lay a new concrete floor. He shovels in the concrete single-handed, smoothing and levelling until everything looks perfect. A few days later, a big stainless steel sink is delivered and Dad plumbs it in himself, then fits a roll of shiny red lino and installs a huge worktable bought on the cheap from Ikea. I never knew my dad could do those things, and even he is looking surprised and pleased with himself.

He gives the walls and ceiling two coats of white paint, and suddenly the whole space begins to look bright and airy and cool.

He still has flecks of white paint in his hair when he puts on his one and only suit to go to the bank and ask about a loan for the chocolate business. Charlotte is going too, of course, looking cool and quirky in a green-print dress with a velvet jacket and jade nail varnish.

Together they look clever and creative and slightly

bohemian, but the business plan Dad has tucked under his arm in a smart black folder is logical and detailed and perfectly planned. The two of them have done their research, and spent every evening over the last week or so putting it all together. There are profit and loss predictions, and artwork samples for the boxes, and a brand-new logo for The Chocolate Box that looks amazing.

If all that does not convince the bank, then the hand-painted box, wrapped with ribbon and filled with freshly made truffles, should swing it.

'We've got a great plan,' Dad says. 'And we've got a pure, dead *brilliant* product. All we need now is one small loan to get us up and running!'

Charlotte straightens Dad's tie and tucks his shirt in for him, I hug them both, and they get into the little red minivan.

'Wish us luck!' Dad grins. Skye and Summer, who have been left in charge of the B&B for the morning, come out on the step to see them off, and Coco wanders over from the direction of the duck enclosure, with four sleek, black runner ducks at her heels, waving.

The only person who doesn't appear is Honey but, of

course, she doesn't wish them luck anyhow. She probably wishes them plague, pestilence and disaster.

The red minivan crunches away across the gravel.

'Good luck!' I yell, waving until they are out of sight.

'I'm keeping everything crossed for them,' Skye says. 'Fingers, toes, eyes . . .'

So much depends on this meeting. Dad and Charlotte need this bank loan to get the chocolate business off the ground, but plans for the Chocolate Festival are rolling forward anyway.

Charlotte has called the organizers of the Food Trail to tell them about The Chocolate Box and the festival. They loved the idea, and agreed to add it to the brochure and the Food Trail map, which have just gone off to be printed. There is no backing out now. Like it or not, on the last weekend in August, Tanglewood will be invaded by dozens of tourists.

'I'm going to paint a banner for the festival,' Skye announces, heading back into the house to unload the dishwasher. 'And we can make bunting and string it all around the garden and set stalls out under the trees. Mum says maybe we can have picnic tables and chairs like a kind of outdoor cafe, and sell hot chocolate with marshmallows and chocolate milkshakes and chocolate ice-cream sundaes . . .'

'We can make our Cherry Chocolate Cola Cake,' Summer says, stacking the crockery away in the dresser. 'That's gorgeous. And Coco can do chocolate fridge-cake, the kind that doesn't need any cooking . . .'

'How about a chocolate fountain for one of the stalls?' I chip in. 'I saw one at the big Thorntons shop in Glasgow, once. People could dip strawberries and marshmallows and things into it. That would be cool!'

Summer grins. 'Brilliant! My friend Evie got one of those for her birthday, I'm sure she'd let us borrow it. I'll ask!'

Once we have tidied the kitchen, we head upstairs to make up two of the rooms for new guests arriving later. Skye and I shake a crisply ironed duvet cover down over one of the quilts while Summer pirouettes around the bedroom with a feather duster.

'Ignore her,' Skye tells me. 'She's obsessed. We started lessons together, when we were four . . . but I didn't last, I was useless. Did you ever do ballet?'

✿✿✿✿✿✿✿✿✿✿✿✿✿✿✿✿✿✿✿✿✿✿✿✿✿✿✿✿✿✿

I blink. 'Oh . . . yeah,' I hear myself say. 'I did it for a while, but I wasn't keen. I gave up a couple of years ago . . .'

Why do I say these things? Stupid, stupid, stupid. The only dance lessons I've ever had were at school, in PE. They used to teach us Scottish Country dances with dodgy names like the Gay Gordons, in the run-up to Burns Night. I was hopeless. I usually got stuck with Frazer McDuff, who had bad breath and clammy hands and glasses that were always broken and held together with Sellotape.

I was so bad that on Burns Night they made me a waitress, handing out plates of brown, speckly haggis to the parents at the class Burns Supper so that I wouldn't have to be part of the dancing display. Kirsty McRae teased me for weeks, so eventually I told her my mum was actually a famous ballet dancer in Tokyo, just to shut her up.

It didn't, of course.

She laughed out loud and told everyone I was a sad little liar. I shudder at the memory.

'What grade did you get to?' Summer asks, twirling into the bathroom with an armful of fluffy white towels. 'I bet you were good! Can you do a *pas de chat*? Or a *jeté*?'

'No!' I bark, a little too quickly. 'No . . . I can't do . . .

well, whatever you said. I never got that far. And I never did any grades. They . . . um . . . don't have them, in Scotland. I think I had two left feet . . .'

'Oh?' Summer says, looking doubtful. 'No ballet grades in Scotland? Are you sure?'

The trouble with telling a little white lie is that one lie has a way of turning into more. You cannot back down. You end up digging yourself deeper and deeper, just to avoid detection.

'Certain,' I lie brightly, plumping up the pillows and smoothing down the duvet. 'It's a totally different system, in Glasgow.'

Summer is leaning on the bathroom door, frowning slightly, and I can see that she has sussed me out. She knows I am lying, and her face betrays her feelings. She is confused, disappointed, faintly annoyed.

I don't really blame her.

When will I ever learn?

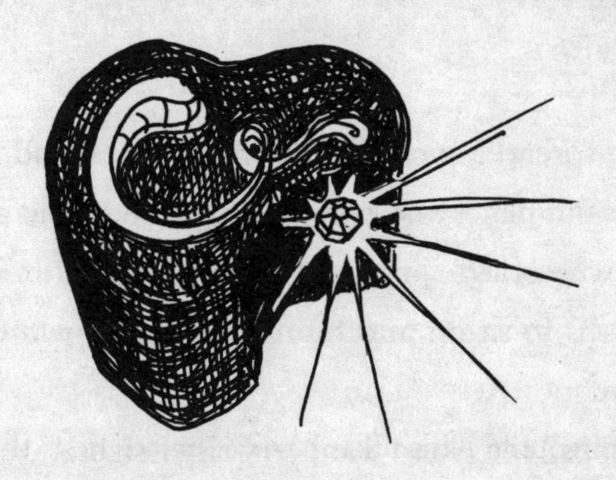

20

The three of us are sitting on the grass in the sunshine, painting a rainbow-bright banner for the Chocolate Festival, when the little red minivan crunches back across the gravel just after one o'clock.

'How did it go?' I call out, running over to the car. 'What did they say?'

Dad looks at Charlotte, and his face breaks into a grin.

'Well . . . I reckon it was the truffles that swung it,' he says. 'But . . . the bank people have approved our business plan! They're giving The Chocolate Box a loan. The business is up and running!'

'We've brought fish 'n' chips to celebrate,' Charlotte announces. 'Go and find Coco and Honey, we'll eat out here . . .'

We spread a picnic cloth on the grass, and Charlotte brings out plates and cutlery and ketchup and a glass jug filled with orange juice and ice. Skye and I run in to fetch cushions to sit on and Summer tracks down Coco and Honey.

'Chips,' the eldest Tanberry sister sighs. 'Well, at least we got something out of it.'

'Got you a couple of pineapple fritters, Honey,' Dad grins. 'Your favourite, right?'

Honey shrugs, unwrapping her chips. The ghost of a smile flickers over her features. 'Yeah . . . I suppose. Thanks . . .'

I have eaten misshapen Taystee Bars on Glasgow Green before, and cheese-and-pickle sandwiches on the steps outside the Gallery of Modern Art, even hot dogs at a folk music festival in the Borders . . . but this is the best picnic ever. Eating chips in the sunshine at Tanglewood House with the Tanberrys, Dad and Charlotte on a high about the chocolate business . . . well, the good mood is contagious. I can almost forget the blunder I made with Summer, with my stupid ballet story. It doesn't seem important any more.

I'm starting to realize that I don't need lies to fit in here, anyway . . . I just need to be me. Maybe that's all I ever needed?

'We're in business!' Dad grins, spearing a chip and dunking it in ketchup. 'The bank thought our plans were really exciting, that we'd researched the project well. All we have to do now is show them they were right to believe in us! I'll get that workshop finished and then we can work flat out to get everything ready for the Chocolate Festival . . .'

'We've got tons of ideas for that,' Skye tells Dad. 'Mum wants to do a chocolate cafe, and we think we can get a chocolate fountain too. I thought I could tell fortunes – you know, dress up as a gypsy or something and sit on the caravan steps and tell people what their favourite truffle would be, a bit like in *Chocolat*!'

'A couple of my friends will probably help out, if we need them,' Summer chips in.

'I don't suppose you'll need me,' Honey says carelessly. 'But . . . if you do . . .'

We all turn to look at her. If we do, what? She'd rather die than get involved in the Chocolate Festival, surely?

'What?' she snaps, biting into a pineapple fritter.

Charlotte laughs. 'Nothing, love . . . but yes, of course we will need you, Honey. You're so organized . . . we couldn't manage without you! If I do try a kind of open-air chocolate cafe, then I'll be stuck in the kitchen sorting all the orders. We'd need someone to keep an eye on things out here, someone reliable.'

Honey raises an eyebrow. 'I suppose I *could* do that . . .'

'Brilliant!' Charlotte says. 'And I was going to ask Shay if he could rig up a sound system, get some music sorted. It's going to be a fantastic day!'

'Hang on,' Dad cuts in. 'There's a little something special I left in the fridge to cool, just in case the bank came up trumps . . . I almost forgot. This is something to celebrate!'

A few moments later, Dad pops the cork from a bottle of Tesco champagne and pours it quickly into the mismatched mugs and glasses we are holding out.

'Here's to The Chocolate Box,' he grins, raising his mug in a toast. 'To the bank, for coughing up with the loan, and to all of you for believing in my crazy idea. You won't be sorry, I promise you!'

'Whatever,' Honey says, but the rest of us raise our

glasses and drink. I have never tasted champagne before, and it tastes like happiness, like cool, fizzy sunshine. The bubbles explode on my tongue and make me want to laugh.

'I wanted to say thank you too,' Dad continues, raising his mug again. 'To all of you, really . . . Skye and Summer and Coco and Honey . . . for welcoming Cherry and me into your family. For giving me – us – a chance. I know it can't have been easy. To Cherry, of course, for putting up with me all these years, for taking a risk on a new life down here, and for going along with my mad schemes . . .'

Dad looks at Charlotte, and his face breaks into a huge grin. 'Most of all,' he concludes, 'I have to thank Charlotte, for bringing the sunshine back into my life, waking me up, making me see that dreams can come true, and that the best things in life are worth working for . . .'

'Slush-y,' Honey complains, but Skye nudges her and she subsides into silence.

That's when it all goes wrong.

Dad puts a hand into the pocket of his suit jacket and fishes out a tiny, ribbon-wrapped box. He opens his palm and offers it to Charlotte. Her eyes open wide and she takes the handpainted box and opens it, carefully. Everyone is watching, everyone is quiet, and a trickle of foreboding unfurls within me, because there is something dramatic, momentous, about the gesture. Something slightly scary.

No, I think. *No, he wouldn't . . .*

Then the box is open and I breathe a sigh of relief because inside there is just a chocolate, a heart-shaped chocolate with a swirl of white on top.

'Oh, lovely!' Charlotte says. 'Thanks, Paddy!'

'He's given her his heart,' Coco says, fluttering her lashes, movie-star style.

'Does this mean they're sweethearts now?' Summer quips. 'Get it? *Sweet*hearts?

'Oh, please,' Honey huffs.

'You have to taste it, Charlotte,' Dad is saying. 'It's a new flavour. I made it especially for you . . .'

So Charlotte lifts the heart-shaped chocolate up, biting in gently, and then she frowns and takes the truffle away from her mouth and looks at it carefully. Time seems to slow as she picks at the chocolate shell, touches the fondant centre with a fingertip, and then I see the glint of gold, the shimmer of diamonds, and I understand.

'Paddy . . .' Charlotte says. 'What the . . .?'

'Oh. My. Days . . .' Summer breathes.

'I'm reading your chocolate fortune,' Skye says slowly. 'And I predict a happy-ever-after . . .'

'Will you marry me, Charlotte?' Dad asks, just in case she hasn't got the message. 'There is nothing I'd like more, nothing that would make me happier . . . and we can all be a proper family. Will you?'

Charlotte puts an arm round Dad's neck and kisses his ear. 'I will,' she says. 'Oh, Paddy, of course I will!'

'That is just soooo romantic!' Summer squeals.

'A wedding!' Coco grins. 'Can I be bridesmaid?'

Charlotte pulls the ring from inside the chocolate heart. 'Oh . . . oh . . . wow! It's beautiful . . . Paddy, thank you!' She is grinning so much her smile could light up the national grid, and everyone starts to clap and cheer. I wonder why I feel so frozen, because I am happy for Dad and Charlotte, I really am . . . but . . . it hurts, all the same.

And I'm not the only one who feels that way.

Honey looks stricken. Her eyes are wide and her mouth begins to tremble, and the hands that cradle her mug of champagne are shaking.

'No,' she says, and her voice is a whisper at first, rising

quickly to an anguished wail. 'No! How can you, Mum? How can you even think of getting married when you already have a husband? Remember? My dad!'

'Hey, hey, Honey . . .' Dad says, holding up his hands in a gesture of peace. 'Calm down . . .'

But Honey is not calm. 'Don't you tell me what to do!' she screams. 'You're not my dad, and you never will be! You think you're so clever, don't you? You talk about being a "proper family" but you can just back off, because we are a family already, and we don't need you for that!'

'Stop it!' Charlotte yells at Honey. 'Stop it . . . please! Why can't you be happy for me? Why can't you accept this?'

'Because it's wrong!' Honey bites out. 'It's wrong! You don't belong here, Paddy Costello! You worm your way in, sweetening everybody up with your nicey-nicey ways, your stupid chocolates . . . but you don't fool me. I see you for exactly what you are. I hate you, OK? I HATE you!'

She jumps up and runs away across the grass, blonde hair flying out behind her.

Dad looks horrified. He has judged it all wrong, got his timing askew. Things were going pretty well, sure . . . but it's still early days. And Honey will need a lot longer than this to even start to accept us. Like forever, maybe?

'Should we go after her?' Summer asks in a tiny voice. 'Talk to her?'

'No,' Charlotte says, her voice a little wobbly. 'Leave her, Summer. Let her calm down. We can't keep running after her, placating her. She's had this family walking on eggshells for long enough, afraid to breathe, just about, in case it upsets her . . . well, I'm sorry, but I can't keep putting my life on hold for Honey. I just can't. Why can't she see that I have feelings too? Why can't she be happy for us?'

Charlotte squeezes Dad's hand, smiling, but her eyes are bright with tears.

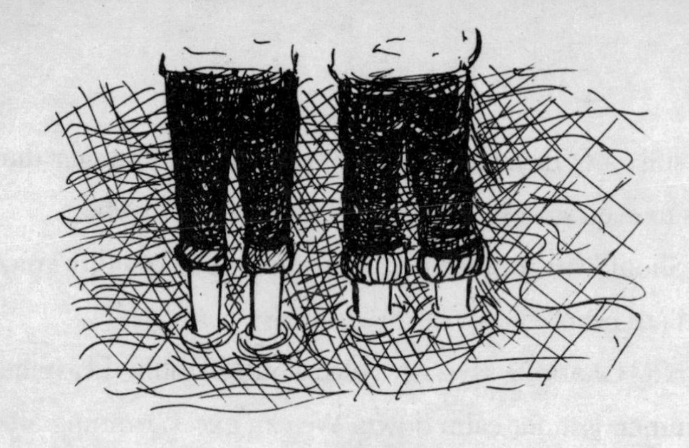

21

The fireworks don't really start until later.

Shay turns up, sunbrowned and smelling of the sea after a day at the sailing centre. Charlotte tells him to tread carefully, because Honey is upset, and Shay just rolls his eyes and shrugs and shoots me the kind of look most people reserve for child-murderers and kitten-stranglers. It's the kind of look that makes me think he is finding this not-being-friends thing as tough as I am, and that he is blaming me for that. It is also the kind of look that says he is tired of treading carefully.

I guess I don't blame him.

Anyhow, Shay and Honey don't appear for tea, and the rest of us are halfway through spaghetti Bolognaise when there's the sound of raised voices and a spectacular slamming of doors.

'Lord,' Charlotte whispers. 'Let's just hope all the guests are out this evening . . . or deaf. What now?'

'Sounds like she's having a go at Shay,' Dad says. 'I hope he remembered his bullet-proof vest.'

'They never quarrel, usually. Shay's so patient . . .' Skye says anxiously.

That's when Shay marches through the kitchen, his face set in a scowl, the blue guitar slung over his back. 'Sorry, guys,' he says. 'I just can't do this right now . . .'

Charlotte gets to her feet. 'Are you OK?' she asks. 'C'mon Shay, whatever it is, it can't be that bad . . . sit down . . . calm down . . .'

But Shay just shakes his head and keeps on walking, slamming the kitchen door behind him.

Much later, walking down to the caravan with Fred, I hear the sound of sad guitar music, so far away it is barely a whisper. I walk past the caravan, down across the lawn, breathing in the scent of freshly cut grass and darkness. No Shay.

And then I hear it again, the sound of guitar in the distance, drifting across the night garden. I creep out through the gate, right to the top of the cliff path, following the sound. Shay is on the beach, a dark figure crouched on the rocks, looking out to sea.

I don't know exactly why I begin to climb down. It's dark and the steps are uneven, and I am supposed to be staying away from Shay Fletcher. But somehow I am on the beach, my feet sinking into soft sand, my hair lifting in the breeze from the ocean.

Shay is sitting on the rocks, his skinny legs folded up in front of him, the blue guitar cradled in his lap. He turns and looks at me, and for once he doesn't seem pleased to see me at all. His face is tight and closed and angry.

'You,' he says tiredly.

I flinch in the moonlight. 'Yeah . . . me,' I whisper.

'Come to laugh?' Shay asks. 'Say *I told you so?*'

'Er . . . not exactly,' I say. 'I was worried about you.'

'Yeah, right.'

Shay chucks his guitar down in the sand.

'I don't know why I bother,' he sighs. 'I try my best to do the right thing, please everybody. I work hard. I see Honey every night. You tell me to stay away from you and I do as you say, even though it's the stupidest idea I ever heard . . . but nobody, nobody, ever bothers about how I feel. What am I, a machine? People can yell at me and tell me I'm rubbish and I just have to stand there and soak it all up? I don't think so!'

Shock and anger curl inside me. I wish I had the courage to reach out to him, the way he did when I was telling my kimono story and got all sad and tearful. I don't, though. I just sit down on the soft sand beside the rocks, shivering.

'Seriously, Honey is one mixed-up girl,' he says. 'She has a mean streak. I'm not even sure what I'm *doing* with someone like that.'

'You love her,' I say, even though the words stick in my throat. 'She's your girlfriend.'

'I don't love her,' he says into the dark, and, in spite of myself, my heart leaps.

'She doesn't even know me,' Shay goes on. 'She never asks how stuff is going in my life. She doesn't care – everything is always all about her. And sometimes . . . well, sometimes I'd like to be able talk about stuff too. You know more about me than Honey does!'

My heart thuds in the darkness.

'So Paddy and Charlotte got engaged,' he goes on. 'Well, good. It's not the end of the world, is it? They make each other happy. Is that a crime? I know Honey is sad about her dad, but surely after three years she should start to accept that the marriage is over? She still thinks he's coming back, and the man can barely be bothered to send her a text half the time. He's an idiot, but she just won't see it!'

Shay tilts his head back and looks up at the stars.

'Anyway . . . Honey's got a plan, the worst plan I ever heard in my life. It's like a kind of blackmail – she wants to make Charlotte choose between her and Paddy.'

A heavy feeling settles inside me, a sense of dread. If Charlotte had to choose between my dad and her own daughter . . . well, that kind of choice is just plain cruel. There could be no happy ending there, not for Charlotte, anyhow.

'She can't do that!' I argue.

'Honey doesn't play by the rules, or haven't you noticed?' Shay says. 'Don't worry . . . I told her it was a lousy idea . . . I don't think she'll go through with it. I hope not.'

He sighs. 'She agreed to put the plan on hold, but she got so angry – told me I was a liar, a loser, a traitor. I'm sick of it, Cherry. I have enough people in my life telling me I'm rubbish . . .'

He gets up suddenly and walks to the water's edge, picks up a flat stone and skims it across the rippling surface. It bounces three, four, five times before vanishing beneath the water. I pick up a stone of my own to skim. It splashes once and sinks without a trace. Skimming stones is not the kind of skill you perfect, living in a place like Glasgow.

Shay skims a few more, then he shrugs and puts his hands in his pockets and we walk along the shoreline together.

He looks like the kind of boy who has had whatever he wanted, from birth, just about. He looks like one of the lucky ones, but I don't think he feels that way.

'Who else tells you you're rubbish?' I ask quietly.

Shay laughs, but it's a harsh, empty sound. 'My dad,' he says. 'My dad thinks I'm useless. He tells me all the time. He hates me – everything that makes me *me*. He has never once been to one of my school nativity plays or concerts. In middle school, I had the lead role in *Grease*, but he said that kind of stuff was for wimps. He hates my music, hates my hair, hates my clothes. Whatever I do, it's never good enough.'

'But you work with your dad,' I say, astonished. 'You teach tourists to sail and you lead canoe expeditions to the smugglers' caves, and take that crazy banana-boat thing out across the bay. He must be so *proud*!'

Shay hunches his shoulders. 'No, he's not proud. He's proud of my brother, Ben – he surfs and sails and plays football, he's tough and strong and practical. He's studying sports and leisure at uni, and he'll probably go into partnership with Dad, one day. Not me. None of that outdoor stuff comes easily to me. Dad knows I hate it, that as soon as I can I will be out of here, to music college, somewhere – anywhere, I don't care, as long as he can't yell at me any more.'

'Oh, Shay,' I sigh. 'I'm sorry. So . . . what will you do?'

He looks at me, and his sea-green eyes rake through my soul the way they did the first time we met. The breath catches in my throat.

'I guess I'll do what I always do,' he says. 'Keep quiet and put up with it. I want a quiet life. I'll keep on slaving for Dad . . . I don't have a choice, do I?'

'And . . . what about Honey?' I whisper.

Shay sighs. 'I feel sorry for Honey,' he says. 'But I don't love her. There are cracks the size of the Grand Canyon running right through our relationship, but sometimes I feel like I'm the only one who can see it. The trouble is, I am a coward. I like it here . . . on the beach, at the caravan . . . at Tanglewood.'

He rakes a hand through the wheat-coloured fringe. 'It feels like home. Charlotte has never made me feel like I wasn't good enough – she accepts me. So do Skye and Summer and Coco. Paddy as well . . . and you. You especially . . . you care. Well, you used to. I don't want to lose that.'

'You won't,' I say softly. 'And I still do care, you know that, Shay.'

'Maybe,' Shay sighs. 'But everything's so messed up now. Honey's threat . . . well, it makes me wonder if I ever knew her at all.'

I don't know where I find the courage, but I take Shay's hand in the dark and tug him down to the water's edge.

'Look,' I tell him. 'It'll be OK. The chances are Honey's all talk anyway, right? Forget it. Don't be sad . . . smile! Let's paddle!'

I kick off my sandals and wade into the moonlit surf. Shay starts to laugh, pulling off his Converse, splashing in after me.

Inside me, a curl of memory unfurls.

'My mum used to tell me to make a wish when I went into the sea,' I say, through chattering teeth, and the words come as a surprise, even to me. 'She said that the ocean would take my dreams and make them real and wash them back up on to the beach . . .'

'Did she?' Shay grins. 'Cool! Let's wish then!'

He holds my hand tight and I close my eyes, and way out there, just beyond my mind's reach, I am sure I can recall this exact same feeling; closed eyes, laughter, a hand holding mine.

I should wish for happiness, for a place I can belong. I should wish for friendship, family, for everything to work out here in Somerset the way I hoped and dreamed.

Instead, I waste the moment on a wish that can never come true . . .

I wish Shay Fletcher was mine.

22

Shay and Honey patch things up, and suddenly it's like Honey has had a whole personality transplant. She starts turning up to breakfast, smiling, chatting, helping Charlotte with the waitressing. She even speaks to me – OK, so it's only 'Pass the jam', but still, it's kind of unsettling.

'She's up to something,' Shay says darkly. 'I don't know what, exactly, but I'm certain she is!'

Skye, Summer and Coco are less suspicious.

'I think it's because she's arranged another trip up to London, to see Dad,' Skye tells me. 'Just Honey, this time. She's travelling up the day after the Chocolate Festival, and staying for three days. They're going to see a West End show, go shopping on Oxford Street, look at the art galleries . . . all of that stuff. Dad wants to spend some quality time with his eldest daughter, apparently . . .'

Summer looks sceptical. 'Since when?' she says.

'Since Charlotte rang and told him Honey really needs some support from her dad, I reckon,' Skye sighs. 'It's not like he'd think of it on his own.'

'Well, it's cheered her up, anyhow,' Coco says.

'Let's hope Dad doesn't cancel this time,' Skye says. 'There'd be no living with her then.'

That's one thing we all agree on.

Temporary or not, Honey's bright mood lifts the cloud that has been hanging over Tanglewood House ever since we arrived. Everything seems easier, somehow, and less of a struggle.

An electrician turns up to help run a power line into the workshop, and slowly the machinery begins to arrive, but Dad stacks it all in the old tack room. Mastering the whole process of making chocolate from scratch is something that will have to wait until after the festival. Instead, he focuses on picking out eight truffle flavours to produce for the festival. No beetroot or curry is involved, but there is a very cool truffle made with cherries from the trees that arch above the caravan.

We pick out names for the flavours – Honey too – and come up with enticing names like Strawberry Swirl and Mocha Melt and Whisky Galore and Cherry Crush. That last one makes me blush, because it's a little too close to the truth.

There is just one week left until the Chocolate Festival, and things begin to get quietly frantic. Charlotte has almost finished the website, and the trees are strung with more fairy lights as well as miles and miles of home-made bunting.

A huge crate of pre-cut and scored card arrives, which Dad and Charlotte decorate with splashes and swirls of acrylic paint. It's Honey's idea to use gold and silver fine-liner pens to add hearts and flowers and stars on top, plus words like *taste* and *dream* and *chocolate heaven*.

'Perfect,' Dad tells her. 'You've got a talent, Honey.'

'Do you really think so?' she asks sweetly. 'Thank you! Whatever I can do to help . . .'

I wonder why I still want to slap her. I must be a very mean and unforgiving person.

I get stuck with putting the painted boxes together, and of course, that is the worst job of all. Skye and Summer and Coco and me spend whole days carefully folding and slotting tabs together, lining them with squares of gold tissue paper and stacking up the finished boxes ready to be filled with fresh truffles on the day of the festival. We cut a million lengths of red ribbon to tie them up with, fold a million colourful brochures telling people about The Chocolate Box and how they can order more truffles over the Internet. It feels like a million, anyhow.

Dad starts working ten-hour days in the workshop, making batch after batch of chocolate fondant, dipping and decorating and freezing everything, ready for Saturday. He looks so happy, so hopeful.

Skye has been working on her chocolate fortune-telling idea. She has filled Rover's old fishbowl with silver foil, crumpled gold tissue paper and lavish handfuls of glitter sprinkles, and turned it upside down so that it looks like a crystal ball.

'I will read their palms and gaze into my crystal fishbowl and tell them which truffles will make them happy,' she explains. 'And then, hopefully, they will go and order tons of them from Paddy!'

'Genius,' I say.

'Should I dress up, do you think?' she puzzles. 'Big hoop earrings and a gypsy scarf?'

Summer looks up from one of her ballet books. 'What about a chocolate-fairy look?' she suggests. 'You could have a cream and brown net tutu with fairy wings and brown satin ballet shoes and a magic wand . . . in fact, we all could. That would be cool!'

'Oh, let's do it!' Skye agrees. 'We could have little brown velvet tops with ribbon straps and gathered net skirts, with the cream and brown net layered . . . I can make something, I'm sure I can!'

'I've probably got enough old pairs of ballet shoes,' Summer grins. 'They're a bit worn, but we'd be dyeing them anyway . . .'

'I've still got fairy wings,' Coco says. 'And there's an old pair in the dressing-up box too. I bet we can borrow the rest . . .'

I bite my lip. I can picture the Tanberry sisters dressed as chocolate fairies, with their tawny-blonde hair and their easy confidence. I just can't quite picture me.

I remember what Honey once said, about me never fitting in here no matter how hard I try.

'What's up, Cherry?' Coco asks, noticing my frown.

'I was just wondering . . . about the chocolate fairies. Do you mean me too?'

Summer rolls her eyes.

'Er, hello?' she says. 'Of course, you too! You think we are going to let you off the hook? We're all in this together, right?'

Summer returns from her afternoon ballet lesson with metres of cream and golden-brown net and soft chocolate-coloured velvet, and we start work right away. Skye makes five little velvet vest tops with ribbon straps and Coco makes five fairy wands from garden sticks painted silver and card-board stars dipped in glitter glue. Me, I end up gathering layers of cream and brown net to stitch on to thick bands of elastic while Summer paints her collection of old ballet shoes with glossy brown dye and stitches on new satin ribbon the colour of chocolate.

'We'll look great!' Skye grins. 'A whole bunch of chocolate-box sisters!'

I think she could be right.

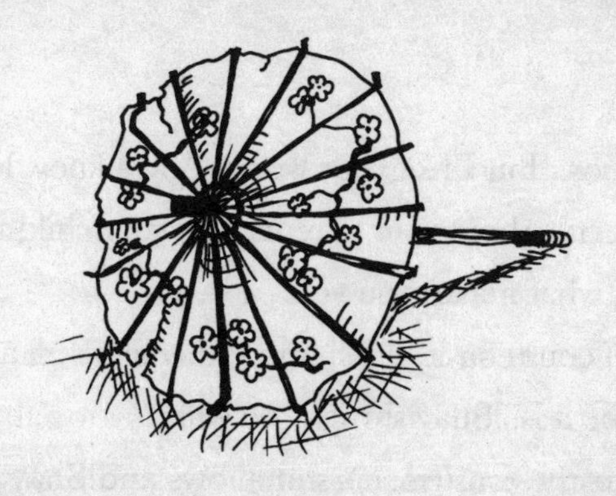

23

I wake to the sound of sad guitar music outside the caravan and the smell of woodsmoke. I push the door open. Shay has lit a tiny, crackling bonfire, and set skewered marshmallows to toast in the embers.

'Hey,' he says.

'Hey.'

'Honey is doing my head in,' he says, turning the marshmallows gently. 'I think I preferred her when she was all strung out and psycho. She is definitely acting weird. Seriously, I'd go nuts if it weren't for you. It's a relief to hang out with someone who isn't living in a fantasy world.'

I almost laugh out loud. 'Me?' I grin. 'You mean me? Honest, Shay, you don't know me at all. I've lived in my own little fantasy world for years.'

✿✿✿✿✿✿✿✿✿✿✿✿✿✿✿✿✿✿✿✿✿✿✿✿✿✿✿✿✿✿✿✿

He grins. 'But I like your world. And I know lots about you, Cherry. About your parents, and your childhood, and . . . well, what makes you you.'

'Don't count on it,' I tell him. 'Maybe it's all a story.'

'Maybe it is,' Shay shrugs. 'So what?'

We eat the toasted marshmallows and Shay plays his guitar some more, and I ask how work is going and he says it's the same as always, which is miserable.

'Dad made me scrape barnacles off the hull of a sailing boat for two whole hours, this morning,' he says. 'I had to paint it too, with this protective paint that stinks like crazy, and then I had to take a whole gang of grockles over to the smugglers' caves . . .'

'I'd like to see them,' I say. 'The caves, I mean. Skye's told me about them, but they're quite difficult to get to by land, aren't they? A steep path through the woods, or something.'

'It's a long way too, on foot,' Shay says. 'I'll take you by boat, one day.'

'I'd like that.'

He hangs his guitar from a tree branch and chucks another log on to the bonfire.

'Do you ever sleep?' I ask him. 'Or do you just work and play guitar and sit by bonfires in the dark? I think you're nocturnal. Like an owl, or a fox or something.'

He laughs. 'I'm going home,' he says. 'I promise. Dad's already losing the plot because I've stayed out late a couple of times. He'd go nuts if I stayed out all night, seriously. He still hasn't agreed to let me help at the Chocolate Festival . . . he seems to think it's some sort of rave, not a gimmick to sell chocolate. You can't explain anything to him.'

'I hope he relents and lets you help . . .'

'He'd better,' Shay sighs. 'Seriously, though, I wanted to hear the rest of your story. What happened to Sakura?'

I wrap the quilt round me in the darkness, and I look into the flames.

'Sakura's dad was unhappy,' I begin. 'He was alone, with a small child to look after. He took Sakura home to Scotland, on a jet plane. Above the clouds, the sky was blue, and Sakura began to hope that there would be colour in her world again – but when they landed, the skies were grey.

'Paddy got a job at the chocolate factory and Sakura

started school, and everything was different. Sometimes, Paddy had to work early shifts, but he was always there in the afternoon to meet her, with a misshapen Taystee Bar in his pocket for them to share.

'One morning, the lady from the flat next door was getting Sakura ready for school. It was raining, and Sakura ran into Paddy's room and took the paper parasol Kiko had used at festival time. The old lady frowned and asked if that was what umbrellas were like in Japan. Sakura said they were, but really she just wanted to feel grown-up, holding the bright painted parasol that had belonged to her mum.'

I sigh. 'Sakura didn't know much about Scottish rain, of course. It soaked the paper parasol, loosening the varnish, softening the paper. By the time Sakura got to school, her face and hands were streaked with red and pink and turquoise paint, and the parasol was ruined . . .'

'Ouch . . .' Shay says. 'What did your dad say?'

'He said it was still beautiful,' I tell him. 'Even though the edges had torn, and the colours had run. The parasol wasn't ruined, he said . . . it had just changed, lived a little.'

Shay laughs. 'Your dad is cool,' he says, and that makes me smile.

'Things were changing for Sakura,' I conclude. 'In Scotland, everyone called her by a different name – Cherry – and talked to her in the language her dad used, never the one her mum had spoken. Slowly, she began to forget. She forgot about Kyoto, and the cherry blossom in the park, and the language everyone spoke and the clothes they wore on festival days. She forgot about the shrines and the pagodas and the neon signs that lit up the city at night. But she never, ever, forgot her mum.'

Shay hugs his knees in the firelight. 'That's beautiful,' he sighs. 'But so, so sad . . .'

I sigh.

When Shay first called round to the caravan, a few weeks ago, the stories were a way of fobbing him off, keeping him at arm's length. A little chunk of story to make him go away . . . it seemed like a fair trade. Things didn't quite work out like that. The stories are too personal, too powerful. They didn't push Shay away, they drew him closer. They have spun a web around us both, and breaking free seems impossible. I don't even want to break free, not any more.

I am tired of fighting this.

I look at Shay and he looks back at me through the firelight, his face lit with flickering orange. I have to look away because my cheeks are burning, and it has nothing at all to do with the fire.

24

The next few days rush past in a blur.

Charlotte borrows crates of cups, saucers, plates and cutlery from the village hall in nearby Comber's Tor, plus ten trestle tables and a whole stack of folding chairs. We set up four tables under the trees on the flat part of the lawn, to make the stalls, and arrange the rest down by the wall so the visitors can have their refreshments while looking out over the beach.

Shay helps Dad to rig up an outdoor sound system, complete with dodgy sweet-themed playlist as promised.

Shay's dad still wants him to work on the Saturday, which is a bit of a disaster. Weekends are the sailing centre's busiest time, he says, especially this particular one, when more tourists than ever flood into the village because of the Food Trail.

'He won't budge,' Shay tells us gloomily. 'I've explained how important this is – but no. I'm not a son, I'm a slave, to him. It sucks.'

'Don't worry, Shay,' Charlotte says. 'We'll manage.'

Everyone is working like crazy.

We finish off the chocolate-fairy dresses and hang them on the top landing, ready for the big day, along with matching wings and wands and shoes. Charlotte makes some simple menus for the outdoor chocolate cafe and handpainted signs with the truffle names and prices. Wind chimes and strings of bells are hung from random tree branches, and an unused sketchbook is turned into a visitor book to collect comments and addresses so we can mail out brochures to happy customers once the big day is over.

Endless trays of finished truffles stack up in the giant fridge in Dad's workshop, and begin taking over the big fridge in the house. Charlotte is baking chocolate gateaux, fudge brownies and mountains of glossy profiteroles, and the rest of us make two big Cherry Chocolate Cola Cakes and enough chocolate fridge-cake to feed the whole of Somerset.

Even Honey joins in. The trip to London to see her dad is going ahead, the coach tickets bought and paid for, her bag packed . . . and that means she is helpful, efficient and almost fun to work with. She takes charge in the kitchen, dividing up jobs and keeping an eye on everything so that we stop messing around and actually begin to produce tray after tray of gorgeous, chocolatey treats.

'Team work,' she says firmly, apparently forgetting that she has not been a part of anybody's team but her own for quite some time. 'And good leadership. Summer, how is that new batch of chocolate melting down? Skye, have you finished the vanilla icing? Coco, can you load up the dishwasher again and stack those plates on the side . . .?'

'What did your last servant die of?' Coco huffs.

'Nothing, you're still alive,' Honey grins. 'Wait a second, Cherry, you've got chocolate on your face . . .'

She wipes my cheek gently with a square of kitchen roll, and I back away slightly, expecting a sharp dig or a nasty comment, but nothing comes. I think I could almost get to like this new, improved version of Honey – if only it didn't make me feel so guilty.

When Honey is nice to me, it makes it a whole lot harder to justify the fact that I am falling for her boyfriend.

The day of the Chocolate Festival dawns sunny and dry. I run up to the house in my pyjamas, wash quickly, eat toast, then go up to Skye and Summer's room to dress.

'It's years since I've dressed up in fairy wings,' Skye says, twirling round in her chocolate fairy tutu. 'I could get used to this!'

She has added a bundle of cream and brown net and a cascade of chocolate-coloured ribbons to her upswept, tawny hair, woven in braids and threaded through with beads and bells and bits of ancient lace. Skye spends her whole life playing dress-up, channelling her own unique raggedy-fairy look.

Summer has a different look, her hair pinned up in a perfect ballerina bun, her shoulders shimmering with body glitter. She wears the velvet and net like a ballet costume, slides her feet into the soft, brown ballet slippers and ties the ribbons neatly, criss-cross fashion.

Coco bursts in, a small whirlwind, waving her wand about dangerously and pretending to change her sisters into frogs.

'Is Honey dressing up?' I dare to ask.

'I think so,' Skye says. 'She said she would . . .'

The door opens and Honey walks in, looking like she has just done a photo shoot for teen *Vogue* with her waist-length hair and her kohl-rimmed eyes and her lazy, effortless confidence. She somehow makes the home-made fairy costume look like it just came off the catwalk.

And then there's me.

I have no memories of dress-up days with pink fairy wings and fluffy feather boas – my dad never thought of stuff like that, and I didn't go to other kids' houses often enough to come across the whole fairy fantasy. In spite of the stories I told Summer and Skye, I have no experience of ballet classes or end-of-term dance productions, either. In the Christmas plays at primary school, I was always a sheep or a donkey, or once, memorably, a shepherd with a striped tea towel on my head and Dad's fleecy dressing gown.

I was the classic misfit kid, always on the outside looking in.

I wish I could admit all that, but it seems kind of difficult after the little white lies I have told. I look at Skye and Summer and Coco, laughing, talking, adjusting net skirts and twirling in front of the mirror. I could tell them the truth, couldn't I? Admit that I never did ballet, didn't have tons of friends, lived in a tenement flat and not a swish apartment. They wouldn't mind, I know that now. They might even understand why I lied.

Then I see Honey, her head tilted to one side, her long hair swishing, and I know that she would never understand, not in a million years.

I push away any ideas of confession and pick up the fairy costume with a sigh.

I am not really a tutu kind of a girl, but when I slip into the dress I can feel the tug of childhood magic just the same. The velvet is soft against my skin, the layers of net light and airy. The borrowed wings tickle my shoulders, and a cloud of silver glitter drifts to the floor as I move.

'I sprinkled the dresses with fairy dust,' Coco explains. 'So they'll be magic!'

I am not a great believer in fairy dust, but I can't help smiling at my reflection in the dressing-table mirror. Skye brushes my blue-black hair up into high bunches, adorning them with satin ribbon bows, Summer helps me to tie the ballet slippers and even Honey rolls her eyes despairingly and leans in to brush silver glitter along my cheekbones.

The girls check their reflections, adjust their wings and run out on to the landing, laughing, waving their sparkly wands around, while I take one last look in the mirror.

I look like I belong . . . and I almost feel that way too.

I can't stop smiling.

'You look OK,' Honey says. 'Really.'

It's probably the best compliment anyone ever gave me.

I run out of the bedroom, wings bobbing behind me, leaving a glittery trail.

25

The sound system is belting out 'Sugar Sugar', an ancient sixties number Mrs Mackie used to play back in Glasgow, as Honey and I walk down across the grass. Shay comes towards us, grinning.

'Hey,' Honey says. 'I thought you were working?'

'I decided to duck out of it,' he confesses shiftily. 'They'll have to do without me for once. Dad will go mad when he susses I've gone, but hopefully he will be too busy to do much about it. I haven't told Paddy . . . he just thinks Dad changed his mind at the last minute . . .'

'Skating on thin ice,' Honey says. 'I like your style.'

'Hope your dad doesn't go too crazy,' I say.

Honey narrows her eyes. 'Why should you worry?' she huffs. 'You don't even know Shay's dad.'

I try not to look guilty. 'No,' I say. 'Sorry.'

'It's OK,' Shay shrugs. 'Don't stress. I'll deal with that when it happens . . . if it happens.'

He cracks a cheeky grin. 'By the way . . . did you know you have fairies at the bottom of your garden? I mean, seriously?'

'Watch it,' Honey teases. 'That information is Top Secret. Tell anyone and I might have to put a spell on you . . .'

'I think you already have,' Shay says, but his eyes snag on to mine, not Honey's. She catches the look and a shadow passes over her eyes, replaced just as quickly by cold indifference.

Panic flutters inside me like a bird's wing beating on glass. The fragile truce Honey and I have built over the last couple of days comes tumbling down, and suddenly I know why Honey and I can never be friends. There is nothing going on between me and Shay Fletcher, nothing but hopes and dreams that will never be anything more. There is definitely nothing anyone could ever see.

Honey sees it, though. I think maybe she has seen it all along.

She snakes an arm round Shay's waist, staking claim,

and drags him away from me, laughing, leaning up to whisper in his ear. I turn away, pink-cheeked.

I find Skye and help her to transform the steps of the gypsy caravan into an oasis of mystical, fortune-telling magic. The chocolate fountain is glugging away gently on a stall nearby. In the kitchen, Charlotte has cleared away all traces of breakfast activity and set out trays, plates, teapots, cutlery, cups, saucers, milkshake and sundae glasses. The counter is crowded with half-a-dozen varieties of chocolate-cake heaven.

At half ten, we take the chocolates from the workshop fridge and carry them down to the stall, arranging them on pretty china plates in towering pyramids. Shay adjusts the music system and Skye and Summer and Coco's friends begin to arrive, ready to help.

Dad puts on a trilby hat he has adapted with cocoa beans dangling on threads from the brim, and ties on a big white apron. I'm just coming out of the kitchen with one last tray of truffles when a blue jeep skids to a halt on the gravel.

A middle-aged man in cut-off shorts and a T-shirt that

says *Kitnor Sailing Centre* jumps out, his face like thunder.

'Where is he?' the man growls. 'I know he's here. Let's face it, he's always here . . . or was. Not any more. That boy has blown it big time . . .'

He looks at me, curls his lip at the sight of my tutu skirt and lopsided wings, and scans around for someone less ridiculous to talk to. Dad appears in the doorway behind me, his arms full of chocolate crates.

'Are you looking for Shay?' he asks politely. 'He's been pure brilliant already, today, helping me to get the sound system running. We're really very grateful you can spare him. He's a great lad!'

Shay's dad turns an ominous shade of purple.

'Are you having a laugh?' he asks. 'He's supposed to be working with me! He had a canoe group booked for ten o'clock. The busiest day of the season so far, and where is he? Up here, with you weirdos, playing that stupid guitar at a bloomin' festival . . .'

Dad blinks. 'Oh, it's not that kind of festival,' he says. 'It's part of the Food Trail, launching our new chocolate business . . .'

'While my business goes down the pan,' Shay's dad says grimly. 'D'you think I care about your poxy little festival? Not exactly mobbed, are you? No . . . but you still need my son to run around doing your errands!'

'He offered!' Dad splutters. 'And we will be busy, I hope . . . we haven't even opened yet!'

'Whatever,' Mr Fletcher growls. 'Let's get this straight, Mr . . . well, you're not Mr Tanberry, are you? Whoever you are. I don't like my son hanging out up here till all hours. Two in the morning he got home, the other night, and that wasn't the first time. Where is he, anyhow? Lazy, lying, useless little layabout . . .'

Shay steps out of the trees. His face is closed and his shoulders slump, and I know right away that he has heard every word.

'Get in the jeep,' his dad says, and Shay gets in, cheeks burning.

'Just hang on a minute, there,' Dad is saying. 'Mr Fletcher, is it? I think there must be some misunderstanding. Shay obviously thought . . . well, I don't know what he thought, but he was only trying to help us! You can't just come up here, yelling and shouting . . .'

'Watch me,' Shay's dad snarls, and he guns the engine and drives away in a spray of gravel.

'Poor Shay,' Dad says.

Poor Shay indeed.

Ten minutes later, Shay texts Honey to say he has been grounded for a fortnight. 'He's not allowed to see me!' she declares, outraged. 'His dad expects him to work every day and sit around at home every night. It's practically inhuman! The man's a monster!'

'He'll probably calm down,' Charlotte says. 'A fortnight might seem like forever, when you're fourteen, but it will pass. It'll be OK.'

'It had better be,' Honey growls.

There's no time to worry too much about Shay or Honey, though, because the first real visitors begin to arrive. I take my place behind the counter with Dad, while Honey and Summer get their notebooks ready to scribble down orders for the outdoor chocolate cafe.

It's the last time I get a chance to draw breath for five whole hours. More and more cars arrive, and streams of tourists begin to wander down across the lawn, and I am seriously glad that Coco sprinkled fairy dust over the brown tutu dresses, because the chocolate fairies need all the help they can get.

I take up my tongs and start picking out truffles, selecting the flavours each customer points to. I get used to folding down the tissue paper, sealing boxes, tying ribbon bows, and I take the money and use the calculator to add everything up, counting the change out slowly. Soon there's a queue, and then a whole crowd, and people aren't just buying one box but two or three.

'These look amazing,' one woman says. 'The boxes are so unusual!'

'They taste even better than they look . . .'

'So pretty,' another adds. 'They'll make the most amazing presents . . . can you do really big boxes too?'

'No problem,' I say. 'We can do chocolates for any occasion . . .'

Skye must have a steady stream of punters for her chocolate fortune-telling, because most of them come down to buy a box of whichever variety she has predicted they will love.

As for the refreshments, Honey and Summer are run off

their feet. The four trestle tables reserved for refreshments are full, and people overflow on to the patio too, balancing their plates and teacups on knees as they flick through brochures and admire the fish pond. When people begin to gather in clumps, waiting for a space, Honey grabs an armful of picnic blankets and spreads them on the grass, and keeps on serving.

You can't even get near the chocolate fountain, and a friend of Charlotte's has to be dispatched down to the village for emergency supplies of fresh fruit and marshmallows.

In the afternoon, Honey appears with a clutch of journalists in tow, and we get a five-minute break while they quiz Dad and Charlotte about the business and take pictures of the chocolate fairies posing with little boxes of chocolates. One is from the local newspaper, but the other works for one of the big national women's mags and is certain she can run a big story about Dad and Charlotte and their chocolate-fairy daughters.

Even Fred gets in the pictures, looking like a small grey-and-white haystack and wearing Coco's fairy wings.

'We're going to be famous!' Skye and Summer whisper together.

'Do you think?' Coco asks.

'I think,' Honey says. 'How cool is that?'

She grins at her sisters, radiant, but her eyes slide past me as if I am invisible.

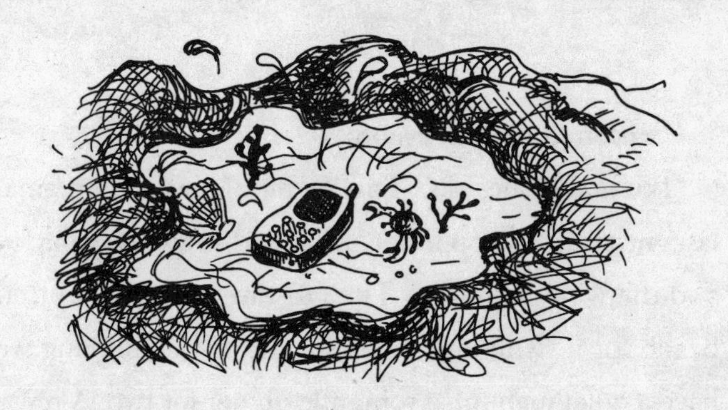

26

A part of me wants the buzz of the festival to go on forever, even when my feet begin to ache and my shoulders sting with sunburn and my wings hang sadly askew, but by five o'clock the last of the crowds thin and dwindle. We start to clear things away, picking up litter and gathering plates and dishes to bring up to the house.

All anyone really wants to do is flop down in a heap and recover, but Charlotte pushes us on.

'Come on,' she says. 'If we get everything cleared now we won't have to do it tomorrow . . . and then we can really relax. OK?'

'You are a hard woman, Charlotte Tanberry,' Dad sighs. 'I don't think I can even stay standing much longer. I'm just about ready to keel over . . .'

Charlotte raises an eyebrow.

'Too tired?' she asks. 'That's a pity. I have a home-made lasagne ready to pop in the oven, and strawberry pavlova, and the wine is chilling. The girls are going down to the beach for a swim and a picnic, and I was thinking we'd have a quiet night in, a romantic dinner for two. A reward for all the hard work of these last few weeks. But of course, if you're too tired . . .'

Dad holds up his hands, grinning. 'Tired?' he says. 'Me? No, not a chance . . . I'm raring to go!'

Charlotte laughs. 'Thought so . . . funny, that! Well, girls, let's get moving, get this place cleaned up!'

An hour or so later, the worst of the chaos is sorted. The trestle tables and folding chairs have been stacked in the workshop, the empty boxes and crates have been cleared away and the washing machine is whirling through a final spin cycle.

Inside, the kitchen table is spread with a fancy white cloth, the CD player is churning out sad Irish fiddle music and Charlotte is lighting candles and setting out two shiny wine glasses. Dad appears in the doorway wearing a clean T-shirt and jeans, his hair still damp from the shower.

'Slush-y,' Honey says, pulling a face.

'We're allowed to be slushy,' Charlotte grins. 'We're engaged, remember? Besides, I think we've earned a night off after all that hard work! And we'll have to be up at half six tomorrow, remember, to start the guest breakfasts . . .'

'Whatever,' Honey says. 'I just wanted to remind you that I'm going up to Dad's tomorrow. You have to drop me at the bus station in Minehead – my coach is at five to nine.'

'Oh, goodness . . .' Charlotte says. 'London, of course. I was forgetting, with all the chaos today. Are you all packed? I know it's only for a couple of nights, but don't leave it to the last minute . . .'

Honey raises an eyebrow. 'Don't stress, Mum,' she says. 'I've been packed for days. I'm the organized one, remember?'

'Too right you are,' Paddy grins. 'You were brilliant, today. I can manage the breakfasts, Charlotte, if that will help . . .'

'OK,' Charlotte says. 'Be ready for eight then, Honey. Now . . . off you go, all of you . . . catch the last of that sunshine and enjoy it! I've packed you up a couple of picnic baskets . . .'

Skye, Summer and Coco come clattering into the kitchen, laden down with towels and swimsuits. They scoop up the picnic baskets, grab crockery and cutlery and tin mugs from the dresser.

'Come on!' Coco nags. 'Let's get down there! Can we take the Irn-Bru?'

'Disgusting stuff,' Honey scoffs. 'Take the lemonade, instead.'

'Take both,' Charlotte says. 'Cherry, can you carry the blankets? And, Honey . . . the picnic cushions are just over there . . .'

The five of us trail down across the lawn, Fred running on ahead, his tail waving madly, and we slip out of the little gate and climb carefully down the path cut into the cliff edge.

We throw down the blankets and cushions, spreading them out across the warm sand. Then Honey's mobile rings, and her voice lights up with excitement.

I can't help biting my lip, a shadow of jealousy darkening my mood. Shay?

'Oh . . . so good to hear from you!' Honey says into her phone. 'Sure . . . sure, Dad . . . I can't wait to see you . . . I'm soooo excited about tomorrow!'

I breathe again. There's no reason why Shay shouldn't

call Honey, of course, but I can't help being glad it's just her dad, probably making last-minute plans for her trip to London tomorrow.

She wanders away to talk.

It's only when Skye, Summer and Coco start wriggling into their swimsuits that I realize I have forgotten mine.

'Fetch it,' Skye tells me. 'No skiving off! Hurry up!'

They run down to the water's edge, yelling and laughing, and I climb back up the cliff path, run across to the caravan and grab up my swimsuit and towel. Picking my way back down the steps again, I can see Honey sitting on a rock in the sunshine, almost hidden beneath the cliff, her golden hair fluttering around tanned shoulders. In spite of everything, there is something slightly lost, alone, about her, as if she is on the edge of things.

The way I used to be.

As I step on to the sand, I look more closely and see that her shoulders are shaking slightly as if she is crying, and my heart stills. It looks like Greg Tanberry has let his daughter down again.

I look over to see if Skye, Summer or Coco have

noticed, but they are far away, out in the waves, swimming, splashing, giggling, floating on the silver-tipped tide.

The only one who can see what's happening is me.

I would like to turn away and pretend I haven't noticed. I'd like to change into my swimsuit and run down into the surf, acting as if nothing at all is wrong, but I can't. I've been there myself, too many times, sad and lost and tearful because I wanted something I couldn't have, a parent who was long gone.

I take a deep breath and walk towards Honey. As I approach, I notice she is talking on her mobile again. Snatches of conversation drift across to me, and I hesitate, unsure of myself.

This time she is talking to Shay, and her tone is so urgent, so pleading, I know I shouldn't be listening.

'Yes . . . I know . . . I know . . . but please, Shay?' she whispers. 'Something awful's happened. Seriously. I need you, I really do! Please?'

She stands up, shakily, snapping the mobile shut carelessly. Then she sees me, and her face falls, and the mobile slides from her fingers and plummets into a rock pool with a satisfying splash.

'Honey!' I blurt out stupidly. 'Are you OK?'

'Does it look like it?' she mutters. 'What do you care, anyhow?'

'Of course I care! You're crying, Honey . . .'

She drags an arm across her eyes, eyeliner smudged and lashes starred with tears.

'I never cry,' she tells me, and I just nod and offer her my swimming towel. She takes it, wiping the streaks of eyeliner and tears from her cheeks, tilting her chin upwards, defiant.

'Has . . . has something happened?' I ask.

'Nothing new,' she says bitterly. 'My dad cancelled out on me . . . again. Something came up, something unavoidable. No, strike that . . . something disastrous, OK? So if I look upset, that's fine, because my dad just dropped the biggest bombshell ever . . .'

She glares at me, and for a moment the mask slips and I see the hurt behind her smoky-blue eyes. It doesn't make her any easier to like, but perhaps a little easier to under-stand.

'A bombshell?' I echo. 'What is it? What's happened?'

Honey pushes a fist against her mouth, shaking her head.

'You think I'd tell you?' she chokes out. 'Yeah, right. You'd like that, wouldn't you? So you could have a laugh at my expense . . .'

'I'd never do that!' I argue, but Honey just rolls her eyes.

'Forget I ever told you anything, Cherry Costello,' she whispers. 'This isn't your business. If you really want to help, just go away, leave me alone.'

I look at Honey, her fairy wings wilting sadly. For a moment, I think I could reach out, put an arm round her shoulders, tell her I want to help, but I know she'd push me away. She doesn't want my sympathy, I can see that.

I turn and walk down to where the picnic blankets are spread out across the sand. I've lost any interest in swimming now. I just sink to my knees and begin to unpack the baskets, setting out pizza, quiche, potato salad, sausages and crusty bread rolls, as well as cake and crisps and fizzy pop.

After a while, Skye, Summer and Coco wade out of the surf and wander over, laughing, grabbing up towels, and Fred bounds after them, shaking himself violently and splattering me with icy water.

'That was fantastic!' Skye declares. 'You missed out, Cherry!'

'I just . . . didn't feel like it, in the end,' I shrug.

'Well . . . there'll be other times.'

'Hey, Honey!' Coco yells, waving over at her sister. 'We're eating! Come on! It'll all be gone!'

'Later,' Honey calls back.

Summer frowns. 'Is she OK?'

I bite my lip. 'I think . . . that phone call . . . maybe your dad cancelled her stay again?' I say. 'She seems a bit upset.'

Skye shakes her head. 'Typical. He always does this! And talk about leaving it till the last minute – this has to be the worst timing ever.'

'She's been in such a great mood too.' Summer frowns. 'Should we go over and say something?'

'I tried,' I say lightly. 'I'm not sure she wants my sympathy, though . . .'

'No,' Skye says with a sigh. 'She'd bite anyone's head off right now, probably. Best let her calm down a bit . . .'

'Suppose she'll come over when she's ready . . .' Coco says anxiously.

We are digging into pizza slices, a little subdued, trying to keep the sausages away from Fred, when Coco shouts out.

'Hey . . . isn't that Shay?'

In the distance, out on the bay, a small figure in a red canoe is paddling in towards the shore. The wheat-coloured fringe and black beanie hat are hard to miss, even at a distance, and a few minutes later Shay is nudging the canoe on to the sand, jumping out and dragging it up on to the shingle.

'Hey!' Skye calls over. 'I thought you were grounded?'

'Honey called me. She says there's some kind of emergency?'

'Dad again,' Summer says. 'Looks like he's cancelled Honey's visit.'

Shay rolls his eyes. 'Right. Well, I made a break for it. Dad went off to the pub with a mate, so I decided to take one of the canoes for a spin . . .'

'You nicked the canoe?' Coco asks, wide-eyed.

'I didn't nick it exactly,' Shay protests. 'It's a family business, after all. Dad's canoe is my canoe, and all that . . . look, I'd better go talk to her.'

He walks across to where Honey is sitting, on the rocks beneath the cliff, and the two of them huddle close, talking intently. At one point, they seem to be arguing, but then Honey nuzzles into Shay's neck, and I have to look away.

✿✿✿✿✿✿✿✿✿✿✿✿✿✿✿✿✿✿✿✿✿✿✿✿✿✿✿✿

We have almost finished eating by the time they wander over to join us.

Honey is trying a little too hard to be bright and breezy, and if she seems slightly brittle as well, nobody mentions it. You would never guess the shine in her eyes came from tears.

'Hey,' I say. 'We saved you some food . . .'

Honey just raises an eyebrow and helps herself to pizza.

'Just so you all know,' she says. 'Dad cancelled my visit. It's no biggie . . . I'd rather stay here anyway, obviously . . . with Shay. Anyhow, Dad said he'd ring tomorrow, after breakfast . . . he wants to talk to you all.'

Summer pulls a face. 'What about?' she asks. 'He never rings, usually!'

Honey shrugs. A flicker of pain flashes across her eyes, but I'm not sure if anyone else notices. 'He's got a new job,' she says. 'But he wants to tell you about it himself. Anyway. Who needs London, right?'

She leans in against Shay, but he edges forward, reaching over for the sausages, as if he hasn't noticed her.

'So tell me, girls . . .' he says. 'How did the festival go? Did you manage without me?'

'The festival was amazing,' Summer tells him. 'Everyone

worked really hard, we sold out of truffles and Mum and Paddy took enough orders to keep us busy for a month at least . . .'

'I told about a million chocolate fortunes,' Skye says. 'And the chocolate fountain and the cafe were mad-busy too . . .'

'We had our photos taken for the papers!' Coco chips in. 'Dressed as chocolate fairies!'

'Yeah?' he grins. 'Well, remember me when you're famous . . .'

Honey laughs and slides an arm round his waist, but Shay pulls back from her slightly and his eyes catch on to mine so that I have to look away. When I glance up again, Honey is watching me with a slightly puzzled look, as though she has missed something but isn't sure what. Guilt twists inside me like poison.

When you look closely, it's not too hard to see the cracks in their relationship, cracks that could break the whole thing apart. That makes me feel anxious and hopeful and guilty and about a million other emotions too, all mixed up together . . . especially now.

I see Honey offer Shay a mug of lemonade and watch

him shake his head and reach out for the Irn-Bru instead. I see him choose mushroom pizza instead of pepperoni, chocolate cake instead of doughnuts, crisps instead of peanuts. Whatever Honey offers him, he wants something different, and when she strokes his hand, ruffles his fringe, he brushes her off carelessly, barely noticing.

Honey notices, though.

'I can't believe your dad has grounded you,' she tells him, trying to corner his attention. 'He is so over the top. I mean, aren't you allowed to have a life?'

'Apparently not,' Shay sighs. 'He thinks I spend too much time up here.'

'You do,' Skye laughs. 'But so what? We don't mind. What was all that rubbish about the late nights, though? Honey's curfew is eleven, and even Paddy and Charlotte hit the hay soon after that, so where he gets the idea you're here till one or two in the morning from . . .'

Shay glances over at me, guiltily, and Honey catches the look. Her eyes darken. Something is bothering her, and sooner or later she'll work it out.

'I told you before, my dad is crazy,' Shay shrugs, a little too smoothly. 'He just invents stuff. What would I be doing anyhow, lurking around till the early hours of the morning? Like you said, Skye, you lot are all asleep . . . and face it, rural Somerset is hardly party central, is it?'

'I suppose not,' Skye laughs. 'It's still pretty cool, though. Cherry was asking me about the smugglers' caves, the other week . . . I told her you were the expert tour guide there, Shay!'

His face lights up, and he grins across at me. 'Oh, I was there today, with a whole gang of grockles in canoes,' he says. 'I'll take you, Cherry, I told you, any time you want to see them . . .'

He trails away into silence, and this time I know that Honey's not the only one to have picked up on his enthusiasm. Shay's cheeks stain with pink and he tries to hide behind his fringe, suddenly awkward. 'Some time, I mean,' he backtracks. 'Maybe. If I can find the time . . .'

The damage is done.

I freeze beneath Honey's glare, hardly daring to breathe, as if staying very still might make me invisible. It won't, of course. Honey looks at Shay and looks at me, and sees what I have been too scared to.

He likes me too.

It's not rocket science. If he'd been any other boy . . . a boy without a drop-dead-gorgeous girlfriend, for example, who just happens to be my stepsister . . . well, I guess I'd have put two and two together by now. Let's just say that maths has never been my strong point.

If Shay likes me the way I like him . . . it's like my best dream and my worst nightmare all rolled into one. Only right now, from the sick feeling that's churning up my stomach, I have a feeling the nightmare may come out on top.

Honey's eyes narrow and she tilts her chin up.

'So, Cherry,' she says coldly, 'you were telling me a while ago about your boyfriend, back in Glasgow . . . and how much you were missing him. When is he coming down to see you then?'

Shock jolts through me, and my heart starts to thump. Honey knows the boyfriend story was a lie, so why bring it up now?

To punish me, of course. If you get on the wrong side of Honey Tanberry, you live to regret it. And how . . .

'Boyfriend?' Shay says, his face pale.

'Boyfriend?' Skye echoes. 'You never told me . . .'

'What was his name again, Cherry?' Honey teases. 'Scott, wasn't it? I asked Paddy, and he said the only Scott he knew of was a speccy little lad who lived downstairs from you in the tenement who was always leaving Freddo bars for you, outside the door.'

My cheeks are burning.

'I don't think so,' I stutter. 'Scott Pickles is only seven . . .'

'That sounds about right,' Honey smirks.

'I think it's a mix-up,' I tell Honey. 'I might have mentioned Scott, and perhaps you . . . um . . . somehow got the wrong impression . . .'

'Perhaps,' she agrees, her voice cool and clear. 'Like when you told me about your luxury penthouse apartment overlooking the Clyde. That turned out to be a titchy tenement flat, which isn't quite the same thing really. And when you mentioned your friends back home and how they'd miss you and be down to visit any moment, which is weird, because as far as I know there hasn't been one phone call, one letter, one single text message from any of them . . .'

She pauses for effect.

'As for Paddy's top management job . . . well, we all

know he used to pick out the reject chocolate bars on the factory production line. You're quite good at giving the wrong impression, aren't you, Cherry?'

Skye and Summer and Coco are staring at me, surprised and faintly embarrassed, but that's nothing compared to how I feel. If I had the courage, I would stand up now, grab Shay's stolen canoe, paddle out towards the horizon and never, ever come back.

I open my mouth to argue, to defend myself, but nothing at all comes out.

'Have you finished, Honey?' Shay says into the silence. 'Or have you got any other nasty, spiteful stuff to share?'

'She's a liar!' Honey snarls. 'Don't you get it, any of you? She's a liar and a cheat and a phoney. She's lied to every single one of you, taken you all in with her stupid stories, can't you see? Don't you care?'

'Just leave it,' Skye tells her sister.

'You're out of order,' Summer says.

'Stop it,' Coco adds, her lip quivering.

'Are you all stupid?' Honey hisses. 'Can't you see what I'm telling you?'

'It wasn't like that,' I protest, but of course, it was exactly

like that. I have twisted the truth to make myself look better, to try to fit in.

'So . . . you didn't really have a boyfriend back home?' Coco asks. 'Or loads of friends, or a posh apartment?'

'You never did ballet, either, did you?' Summer says. 'I knew that wasn't right.'

'I wanted to fit in,' I sigh. 'I thought you'd like me better if you thought I was . . . well, a bit more interesting.'

'We liked you anyway,' Skye says quietly. 'You didn't need to make stuff up.'

Shay sighs. 'Sometimes, people make mistakes,' he says softly. 'They dream so much they get the dreams mixed up with reality. Cherry didn't mean any harm.'

Honey laughs, a sad, harsh sound.

'You think she's so great, don't you, Shay?' she says disgustedly. 'She's really got you fooled. How come you're getting so wound up about Cherry anyway? How come you're defending her? She's not your girlfriend, Shay, or have you forgotten that?'

Shay looks away, and that's when the last shreds of hope die in Honey's eyes. She looks at me and she looks at Shay and the final pieces of the puzzle fall into place.

She turns to her sisters. 'You know what's been bothering me?' she asks. 'It's finding out that my so-called boyfriend has been staying out till one or two in the morning. He hasn't been with me till that time, so where was he? I'll tell you, shall I? Hanging out with Little Miss Perfect here. Am I right, Cherry? Shay?'

I cannot meet her eyes, and that's all the admission of guilt Honey needs.

'Whoa,' Coco breathes.

'No way,' Summer says.

Skye looks alarmed. 'She wouldn't,' she says. 'Tell her, Cherry. It's a mistake, right?'

I hang my head, silent, ashamed.

'It wasn't like that!' Shay snaps. 'We're just friends!'

Honey's eyes flash with anger. 'Shut up, Shay,' she says. 'Haven't you done enough?'

She snatches up Shay's mug of Irn-Bru, hand shaking, swinging it upwards towards his face. I reach out to grab her hand, but all I do is knock her off course, and a perfect arc of orange fizz flies right into my face, cold and sweet and shocking. I cough and splutter and hide my face in my hands.

I think of Kirsty McRae with macaroni cheese sliding down her face, and I want to cry.

Honey looks stricken for about a split second. 'You idiot! You made me do that! And I get all the blame, which is just the way you planned it . . .'

And then her hand flies up and slaps my cheek, and I gasp with the shock and the sting of it, and my eyes well with tears.

'I hate you, Cherry Costello,' Honey yells, 'you've been trying to push me out since the minute you got here. You nearly managed it too . . . As for you, Shay Fletcher, get out of my life. I don't need you, and I don't want you.'

She looks around, her blue eyes flashing. 'It doesn't much matter now, I suppose, but I wasn't just planning to go up to Dad's for a visit. I was going to stay. For good. I'm obviously not wanted here . . . by any of you. Typical, though, even that has fallen flat. Lucky me, huh?'

She jumps up, dragging off her fairy wings and throwing them down on the sand. Coco is crying now, and Summer and Skye are hanging on to their big sister's arms, telling her to wait, to calm down, to listen. They tell her that they love her, that nobody could ever push her out, or replace her, that they'd die if she left Tanglewood to live in London.

Honey isn't listening to anyone. She breaks free and runs towards the cliff path, the house, her sisters close behind. Poor Fred bounds after them, barking and whining.

Shay picks up a beach towel and dabs my face, wiping the sticky drips from my cheek. 'Are you OK?' he asks.

I nod, but I am not OK. I am not sure I will ever be OK again.

'Look . . . I'd better go after her,' Shay says. 'She's obviously hysterical . . .'

Humiliation sticks in my throat, sharp and painful, and it's all my own fault.

I watch Shay climb the cliff path, pausing at the last minute to look back over his shoulder, frowning.

'It'll all work out, Cherry,' he says. 'I promise.'

And that's when I know Shay is a liar too.

27

Some people never learn.

I told myself I would stop the lies, yet still they slid off my tongue like syrup, sweet and sticky, seeping everywhere. All I wanted was to fit in, but the lies backfired, just like always, and ruined everything.

I think of the mad gypsy lady from the post office with her talk about choices, and I know I made the wrong one, over and over. It was always plain and simple . . . a new mum, new sisters, a future . . . or Shay. It should have been no contest, yet still I messed it up.

I was greedy, I wanted it all.

I am the liar, the outsider, the girl who broke up Honey and Shay . . . except of course that Shay went running after Honey. Why am I not surprised?

I am not sure if I can survive this.

I'm an idiot. I thought I was fitting in, doing OK, but all the time I was kidding myself. Charlotte will never be my mum. Skye, Summer, Coco and Honey will never be my sisters . . . the minute I fell for Shay Fletcher, I threw all of that away.

I have never had a family, not one I can truly remember. I just have a bunch of muddled memories and a big hole in my heart where my mum should be. I thought Dad loved me enough to make up for that, but I'm not sure any more.

I can't bear to think about what Dad will say when he finds out what I have done, that I have smashed up the new life he has tried so hard to build for us. I wanted a family, but right now I have never felt more alone in my life.

I see the 'stolen' canoe hauled up on to the sand and I grab it and drag it down to the water's edge. I could point it towards the setting sun, vanish without trace, the way my mum did.

'Hey!' Shay yells from the cliff path. 'Hang on, Cherry! What are you doing? Wait!' Shay yells. 'Wait for me!'

I push the canoe into the waves. Shay is the problem, of course. Waiting for him . . . that won't solve a thing. He is running across the sand, and suddenly all I want is to get away from him, away from here.

I wade into the icy water in my brown-dyed ballet slippers. I have never been in a canoe before. The whole thing dips and tilts and lurches to the side, flooding with water as I scramble in, my fairy dress dripping. I grab the paddle and push down, shoving the canoe away from the shore, but Shay is faster.

He runs right into the water, takes the paddle from me, steadies the rocking boat.

'This is crazy,' he says. 'Come back on to the beach with me.'

'I can't,' I say, and the tears are streaming down my cheeks. 'I won't. I've tried so hard, Shay, but I've wrecked it all . . . I just want to get away. Please . . . I have to . . .'

'Cherry, don't be stupid,' he reasons. 'It's getting dark, and nobody takes a canoe out on the sea at dusk . . . it's way too dangerous!'

'I can't stay here!' I wail. 'Don't you understand? I want

to find a desert island or a magical land where everyone is happy and nobody hates me. I want to float right out to sea and let the currents take me across the oceans to Japan. Or maybe just hide out in the smugglers' caves for the rest of my life! I am running away!'

Shay's face creases with doubt, and then, so fast I barely have time to work out what's happening, he scrambles into the canoe behind me, propelling us forward.

The little boat wobbles and bobs and we move smoothly, silently, away from the shore.

'Let's get one thing straight,' Shay says as he swings the paddle from side to side in a slow, steady rhythm. 'We are not running away. We are just taking a trip by canoe, a short trip, right? Maybe ten minutes, seriously. Any longer and Charlotte and Paddy will notice we're gone and start to panic.'

'Shay, they won't even notice,' I sigh. 'They have enough drama on their hands right now to last most couples a lifetime. So much for the romantic dinner for two . . .'

'Whatever,' Shay says. 'I am in charge of this boat, though, and what I say goes . . . we are not running away. Or if we are, then just for ten minutes. Right?'

'I suppose . . .'

There is no sound for a while except the steady dip and slosh of the paddle. The water is calm and the light is fading and everything is peaceful, but there's a feeling of adventure, of danger almost, too. A canoe is not the most stable boat in the world, I realize. If I shift my weight to one side, it tips and wobbles. If I drag my hand in the water, it stalls and shudders. Even when I am sitting perfectly still, leaning a little against Shay's legs, the gentle rock and roll of it goes on, reminding me that we are not on dry land, but at the mercy of the ocean.

'I like it,' I tell Shay. 'Canoeing. I never tried it before, never thought it would be so . . . free.'

'I suppose,' Shay says, and I remember that it's just another part of being told what to do, for him, and not about freedom at all.

Above us the sky is darkening, but we are not far from the darker stripe of shoreline to our left. A new moon, a perfect sliver of light, glints above us, dusting the tiny waves with silver.

My worries melt away like snow in summer. Darkness fills up all the corners where fears and troubles lurk, paints over the shabby, imperfect world around us. It wraps a cloak of mystery and magic around everything.

I could happily stay right here forever, drifting and floating under the velvet sky, but Shay breaks the silence.

'I'm going to turn round,' he says softly. 'Get you back home. It's too dark now . . . I thought we might get as far as the caves, but the light is against us and I can't tell exactly where we are. It's not safe, Cherry . . . my dad would have a fit if he knew what we were doing.'

Shay dips the paddle and steers us round. The canoe tilts a little and then we are turning, but something is pushing us back, and Shay swears under his breath. 'There's a current . . . that's weird . . . we must be further along than I thought. And closer to the shore. Hang on, Cherry, I need to get us out of here . . .'

'It's OK,' I say dreamily. 'We're fine . . .'

'No,' Shay says, and his voice is sharp, anxious. 'We're not fine . . .'

He scoops the paddle down furiously, and the canoe turns again, but the current tugs us back, pulling us inland, and I cannot see because the sky is velvet-black and the moon is too new, too skinny. And then something scrapes along the bottom of the canoe, and we stop suddenly, jarringly, and a rush of water floods in around us. There is a crunch of splintering wood as the paddle snaps, and then we are tilting sideways, into the icy water, into nothingness.

28

I learnt to swim when I was six years old. Dad took me every week to the pool, sat in the gallery and waved and gave me the thumbs-up every time I got something right. I loved that pool, the smell of chlorine, the lights, the warm, turquoise water, but it is a million miles away from this cold, cold ocean that wants to shock me, numb me, drag me under.

'Rocks,' Shay gasps, behind me in the water. 'Be careful . . . but if we can get to them . . .'

My shin scrapes against something hard and jagged, my hands slide across seaweed slime, barnacles. I haul myself up, slithering, and Shay is beside me, scrambling over the rocks, dragging me with him.

It takes forever to crawl across the rocks and on to dry

land. It's dark, and they are slippery and sharp and some of them jut up out of the water and some are underneath, so we cling on, edge sideways like crabs, plunge down into arctic water and climb out again and again, hands shaking, blue with cold.

'Keep talking,' Shay's voice says in my ear. 'Keep going, don't give in . . . not far now. Not far . . .'

'I . . . I can't . . .'

'Keep talking,' he insists, behind me in the darkness. 'Tell me about Sakura, when she was little, in Japan . . .'

'Sakura . . .' I echo, but my teeth are chattering and my bones are filled with ice, my fingers frozen. 'I can't remember . . .'

'Remember the cherry blossom,' Shay says. 'And the kimono, and the paper parasol. Keep remembering them . . .'

So I try, but everything gets unravelled in my mind and all I can think of are long evenings in the flat in Glasgow, curled up on the sofa with Dad, eating chips and watching telly, with Rover staring glassily from his bowl on the window sill. No cherry blossom, no kimono, no paper parasol, just a drizzly playground and me standing on the edge of a group of girls . . . the faces change over the years, but always I am on the edge.

Clinging on to an especially slimy rock, I lose my grip and slither downwards, grazing my arm, scraping my face. I am waist deep in water again, and cold, so cold I just want to curl up and die.

A cool hand takes mine in the darkness, pulls me up again, and an arm slides round me, hauling me on. Just for a moment, I imagine I really can smell cherry blossom, the whisper of warm breath in my ear, saying words I can't quite hear . . . and then it's gone and I am on my own again.

There is nothing but the salt taste of the ocean, the seaweed smell of the night, the swish of waves and the sound of Shay behind me, clambering across rocks, telling me to keep going, because I am doing great.

'We're there,' Shay says, at last, and he takes my arm and we splash through the shallows and on to the sand, safe.

But I am not sure where *there* is, because this thin spit of damp sand, fringed by sharp, black rocks and tucked beneath a towering cliff, is not the bay beneath Tanglewood House.

'Smugglers' caves,' Shay says, reading my mind. 'We made it after all . . .'

I stumble down on to my knees, exhausted.

'Shay, I'm sorry,' I tell him. 'This is my fault . . . we're going to be in so much trouble . . . the canoe . . . your dad . . .'

'My fault,' he corrects me. 'I should never have come over, never have nicked the canoe . . . never, ever, taken you out in it. I must have been crazy. If we ever get out of this, I will be grounded for the rest of my life, I bet you.'

'Till you're ninety-three,' I joke, although I feel more like crying than laughing. 'Then maybe you can get out just for special occasions, like the pensioners' Christmas party and the whist drive and stuff . . .'

'What is a whist drive?' Shay wonders.

'You may never know,' I sigh. 'Not now you're grounded.'

He shakes his head in the darkness. 'I should have known better, seriously . . . it's a basic rule. You never, ever, take a canoe out after dusk. And you never, ever, take one without wearing a proper life jacket . . . sheesh, I can see why now.'

'We could have drowned,' I whisper.

'We didn't,' Shay tells me. 'We didn't, OK?'

'So . . . how do we get out of here?'

Shay sighs. 'There is no way out, not in the dark. The cliff path is too dangerous, it was closed off years ago . . .'

Shay takes his mobile from his pocket, flicks it open and sighs.

'Dead. Looks like we'll just have to wait . . .'

We cannot even let people know we are safe. I feel sick when I think how close we have come to disaster, sick to think that things could have ended very differently.

'How will they find us?' I ask. 'How long d'you think it will be?'

'I don't know,' he says. 'Could be a while.'

He pulls me to my feet again and we walk up to the foot of the cliffs, find the cleft in the cliff face where smugglers came, long ago, to hide their whisky and tea and silk and cotton bales.

Shay steps inside, and I follow.

My hand brushes against something in the dark, and I jump out of my skin, just about. Shay explains that the cave is all set up with barrels and bales and a life-size model of an eighteenth-century smuggler in a fusty old cloak with a pistol in his hand.

'Great,' I say. 'Just great . . .'

There is nothing to do but wait. We sit down on the floor of the cave, our backs against the wooden barrels. I am beyond cold, so frozen I could cry. Ice runs through my veins and the tattered fairy dress clings to me, soaking, the wings just mangled wire and dripping net. There is no trace left of fairy dust, I know that much. I cannot feel my hands and feet, but the feeling is coming back to the rest of me and I know my shins are bruised and bleeding, the skin torn away, the flesh oozing and sore, crusted with salt and sand. I don't even care.

Shay drags the scruffy old cloak from the shadowy smuggler mannequin, wrapping it round me in the dark. I huddle into it, but still I can't stop shivering, not until Shay puts an arm round me and pulls me close, and then I don't care about anything else, anything else at all.

You have to huddle close, I know, to stay warm, to conserve body heat. It's what climbers do when they are stranded in the snow, what Arctic explorers do when a blizzard strikes and they are down to their last few rations, what shipwrecked sailors like us do.

I know that . . . I'm just not sure if you are supposed to hold hands tightly and press your cheek against the other person's chest so close you can hear their heart racing. Maybe you are. Maybe that is normal. Maybe it is normal for the other person to put his mouth against your ear so that you can feel his breath, warm against your skin.

Maybe.

I am not sure about the kissing, though.

I think that's just us.

When Shay lifts my chin and kisses my mouth, the whole world spins away and I forget everything bad that ever happened to me. I forget the wreck and the fight and the hurt and confusion, and Kirsty McRae's mean little face and Honey's slap and the way I have always been on the outside, on the edge. I even forget the other thing, the thing I never allow myself to think about, the ache inside that never goes away.

We kiss for a long time, and when we stop I am warm and breathless and my heart is racing so fast I don't know if it will ever slow down again.

Shay strokes my face in the darkness, gentle fingers tracing my eyelids, my nose, my lips.

'I have to tell you something,' I whisper. 'Something important.'

'Yeah?'

I take a deep breath. 'All those stories I told you . . . about my mum, about the cherry blossom, the kimono, the parasol, the postcards . . . they weren't true. My mum died when I was four. She had a heart condition, and nobody knew, and she just . . . died.'

'Oh, Cherry,' Shay says into my hair.

'It was awful. I didn't understand, and Dad wouldn't talk about it. If I tried to ask he'd get so upset . . . I just stopped asking, in the end. I started to wonder if I'd got it wrong, if my mum was still alive, somewhere else . . . it got so I couldn't be sure what was true and what was make-believe.

'I don't have any real memories of my mum, Shay. No special festival in Kyoto, no kimono, no parasol. Mum and Dad travelled before I was born, but they settled back in Glasgow, and that's where I've always lived . . .'

'It doesn't matter,' Shay whispers. 'Not to me.'

I sigh. 'I got the fan as a Christmas present when I was seven, and I found the kimono and the parasol in a charity shop in the Byres Road, last year. They made me feel closer to my mum, somehow . . . they were the kind of things she might have given me, if she'd had the chance . . .'

Shay strokes my hair.

'The kimono never smelt of cherry blossom, just moth balls and charity shops. No wonder Honey threw it out of the window. And the parasol was always broken, with the colours all running into each other. They were all just stories, lies. I think I do remember something about the cherry blossom, but I can't be sure – and the park would have been in Glasgow, not Kyoto. I'm sorry, Shay.'

'I knew they were stories, Cherry,' he tells me. 'Paddy told the Tanberrys right at the start that your mum had died, and I kind of knew you'd never been to Japan. I didn't know I was supposed to believe it all . . . I just loved listening. They're great stories . . . you should write them down. It's a skill, to weave a fantasy like that . . .'

A skill? Back in Glasgow, my classmates and teachers were not so easily impressed. I remember Miss Jardine's suggestion that I see a counsellor, the way my classmates raised their eyebrows and turned away when I told them tall tales of my mum's exploits in New York, Paris, Tokyo. They called me a liar, and I knew they were right. I told lies, invented stories, to fill up the big hole in my heart that was left when Mum died.

It never quite worked, somehow.

'Shay . . . do you think Honey was really planning to stay in London with her dad?' I ask into the darkness. 'Never come back?'

'Maybe,' he says. 'It sounds like a part of that whole blackmail thing she mentioned a while ago. A way of making Charlotte choose between her and Paddy . . .'

'And now it's all fallen through,' I sigh. 'No wonder she took it hard.'

Shay frowns. 'Earlier on, when I was talking to her alone, she kept saying it was all over, that everything was ruined, that she'd lost her dad too . . .'

'Poor Honey,' I sigh.

'Yeah, poor Honey,' Shay says. 'I feel sorry for her . . . but I can't keep pretending I want to be with her, Cherry, because I don't. I can't. We're supposed to be this perfect couple, but it's never been that way . . . we were only ever marking time, making do. I don't even know why she picked me out . . . maybe because I was familiar, because her friends liked me? Girls seem to think I'm good-looking, or something . . .'

I cannot let that go.

'Modest, aren't you?' I say, jabbing him in the ribs with my elbow. 'Have you seen yourself, lately? The words *drowned* and *rat* spring to mind.'

Shay laughs. 'My famous charm never has worked on you, has it?' he grins. 'I think that's one of the things I like about you! There's an honesty about you . . .'

My eyes open wide in the darkness, but Shay is not winding me up.

'Seriously,' he says. 'It's like I really know you. I know about what happened to you, and other stuff too . . . your hopes and dreams, all of it. Honey is different. She never gives a single bit of herself away. She can't, because she's still all cut up about her dad. I think she's gonna go right off the rails, any day now. I just don't want to have to be the person who picks up the pieces. Not any more.'

I squeeze Shay's hand in the darkness.

✿✿✿✿✿✿✿✿✿✿✿✿✿✿✿✿✿✿✿✿✿✿✿✿✿

'It's you I want to be with, Cherry,' he says. 'I can't help it. I've felt this way ever since I first saw you.'

I smile, because I know that now. Perhaps I knew it all along?

'I'll tell Honey as soon as we get out of here,' Shay is saying. 'I'll explain so she doesn't blame you, so she understands . . .'

My smile fades. I know this is something Honey will never understand, or forgive. There is no future for me and Shay, no future here for me at all . . . and no amount of make-believe can change that.

29

When I wake, the dawn light is seeping through the cave entrance, yellow tinged with pink. Shay's arms are round me and his head is heavy on my shoulder, the two of us wrapped in the scratchy grey cloak borrowed from the smuggler mannequin, who looms over us now, wild-eyed and brandishing his fake pistol menacingly.

I can hear the whir of a motorboat in the distance, and I nudge Shay awake. 'People,' I say. 'Someone's here. I think we are rescued . . .'

Shay jumps up, pulling me to my feet, and we run out on to the sand. In the daylight, we look like ghosts or refugees or shipwreck survivors, which of course I suppose we are. Our clothes damp and tattered, our arms and legs cut and bruised and bleeding, our eyes dark with exhaustion.

'Hey,' Shay says with a weary smile. 'Miss Robinson Crusoe.'

'Hey,' I grin. 'Man Friday, right?'

'Right.'

In the distance I can see a little white motor launch bobbing over the silvery ocean, and Shay and I start to wave, yelling until our voices are hoarse.

The little boat has seen us, though, and it nudges in towards us, running ashore in the shallows. Shay's dad, grim-faced, jumps out with Paddy at his heels, the two of them splashing towards us, and the next thing I know Dad has me in his arms, lifting me up and whirling me round and round.

'Don't . . . ever . . . do that to me again!' he says into my hair. 'I swear, Cherry, I couldn't stand it. I lost your mum . . . I can't lose you. Not ever!'

'You won't,' I tell him.

Dad lifts me into the boat and I look back at Shay and my eyes open wide. His dad is hugging him, hard, the big, gruff, grumpy man and the skinny, rebellious boy. He claps him on the back and when they break apart I see Shay's dad drag a hand across his eyes, take a deep breath in.

Shay clambers aboard, chucks me a life jacket and puts one on himself. He looks grey-faced, weary. His fringe is a sad veil of damp rat's tails, but the beanie hat is still in place, slightly askew.

Dad moves astern, making mobile calls to the police and the coastguards and Charlotte, while Mr Fletcher guns the engine. The little motor launch noses out of the bay, chugging carefully between the long lines of black rocks we crawled over last night.

I feel sick just looking at them.

'You don't need me to tell you how stupid you've been, right?' Shay's dad barks. 'You can see that, can't you? Do you know how many shipwrecks there have been in this cove, back in the smuggling days? How many people lost their lives trying to steer round the rocks in the dark?'

Shay hangs his head.

'It was my fault,' I say in a small voice, and Shay takes hold of my hand and holds it tightly.

'Well, you're safe now, and that's what matters,' Mr Fletcher says, turning back to his wheel. 'Thank God.'

Shay looks at me from under his fringe. 'Did I hear that

right?' he whispers. 'Who is that guy, and what's he done with my dad?'

'He loves you,' I say.

For once, Shay doesn't argue.

'They found the canoe,' he tells me. 'Floating upside down, a little way out from Kitnor Quay. They must have thought . . .'

I don't even want to imagine what they must have thought.

'We were worried sick,' Dad says. 'It was dark by the time we realized you were missing, and we looked everywhere. Then someone remembered the canoe, and we ran down to the beach and it was gone . . .'

'It was my fault,' I tell him. 'Not Shay's. I was upset . . . I thought everything was ruined . . .'

'Nothing is ruined,' Dad says. 'Not now we know you're safe. Last night was pretty dramatic, though. The girls told me what happened down at the beach . . . the things Honey accused you of . . .'

He looks at the two of us, his eyes questioning.

'We didn't plan it,' Shay says. 'We didn't mean to hurt anybody.'

I just wrap my arms around myself, shivering, shame-faced.

Dad sighs. 'Thing is, there was a reason why Honey jumped off the deep end – quite apart from whatever was or wasn't going on with you two. She had a phone call from Greg . . .'

'Oh, yeah,' Shay says. 'Her dad cancelled out on her again, and she took it pretty hard. I know. That's why she called me, asked me to come over . . .'

Dad still looks troubled.

'We think,' I say uncertainly, 'that Honey might have been planning to stay in London with her dad. For a while, anyway. That's why she was so gutted, right?'

'Yes, she mentioned that . . . but there was a bit more to it,' Dad says, frowning. 'Greg has just been offered a new job – in Australia. It's one heck of a bombshell to drop on anyone, especially over the phone, but . . . well, that's his style, from what I've seen. He always takes the easy way out.'

'Australia?' Shay repeats. 'No way . . . poor Honey.'

I didn't think it could be possible to feel any worse, any more guilty, but boy, was I wrong. I think back to yesterday at the beach, to Honey's lost look, her tears, her anger. She mentioned a bombshell, a disaster . . . she even told her sisters that their dad would be calling them, to tell them about his new job. Now I know why.

A dad who calls you on your mobile to explain that you cannot come and live with him because he's about to move to the other side of the world . . . well, that has to hurt. The stuff about me and Shay must have been the icing on the cake.

'The girls were in pieces, obviously,' Dad goes on. 'It was chaos. And in the middle of it all, we discovered you two were missing . . .'

'I'm sorry,' I whisper. 'I've wrecked everything, haven't I?'

Dad slides an arm round my shoulder and pulls me close.

'We can sort this out,' he tells me. 'It's one heck of a mess, sure, but . . . well, we'll deal with it. That's what families do.'

'But Charlotte . . . and Skye and Summer and Coco . . .' I protest. 'They won't want me now!'

'Want you?' Dad echoes. 'Of course they want you. They're worried sick about you!'

We sit in silence until the little motor launch slows and turns, swooping into the bay beneath Tanglewood House.

Charlotte and the girls are waiting on the beach, looking almost as tired and grey and weary as we are. They wave and yell and run down to the water's edge as the little boat chugs in, all except for Honey, who stands alone, watching, further up the beach.

Her cold blue eyes slide over me, over Shay. She sees his hand, curled round mine, and understands instantly. Just for a moment, her eyes flicker with hurt, betrayal, and then they are icy cool again.

I get up to clamber out of the boat, and Shay stands too, to help me. At the last minute he pulls me close in a quick, warm hug, the boy I've been crushing on for weeks, the boy with the cool blond fringe and the blue guitar, the boy who smells of darkness and the ocean.

'Be brave,' he whispers into my ear. 'It'll all work out.'

The hug says more than any amount of words ever could, of course. It makes everything clear, and I know there can be no going back to the way things were before.

We break apart, and everyone is staring – Honey, obviously, and Dad and Mr Fletcher and Charlotte and Skye,

Summer, Coco. Their faces register shock, surprise, dismay, amazement . . . except for Honey's, which shows nothing. No pain, no anger, no emotion at all.

She turns sharply and walks away.

I sleep right through the day and into the evening, and when I wake a doctor is there to check me over, and he says I am fine, just a few cuts and bruises, no lasting damage. Sleep, he says, will be the best remedy. And after the doctor a couple of policemen, who sit at the kitchen table and lecture me gently on the foolishness of running away and taking a boat on the water in the dark. I listen and I hang my head and tell them I will never do those things again as long as I live, and I mean it, I really do.

Once the policemen have gone, we eat tomato soup that Charlotte has made specially, because Dad told her it was my favourite. I eat it and I do not mention that the kind of tomato soup I love best comes from a tin, and is best eaten with white sliced bread and margarine, not the multigrain rolls Charlotte has baked and spread with butter.

Honey doesn't join us at the table.

'I'm sorry about your dad,' I tell Skye and Summer and Coco. 'Really sorry.'

'It sucks,' Skye says. 'He's pretty useless, as dads go.'

Charlotte sighs. 'Greg couldn't have chosen a worse way to break the news, or a worse moment . . . but yes, it's typical of him. Why he couldn't just come down here for once and explain it all properly . . .'

I take a sip of soup.

'Is it all over with Honey and Shay then?' Coco asks. 'Are you his girlfriend now?'

I blink. 'I don't know. Maybe.'

'I thought you hated him?' Skye says, frowning.

'I thought I hated him too . . .'

Summer says what nobody else dares to. 'Honey's furious. She's been locked in her room all day, crying and playing her music too loud. She won't let anyone in. Not me, not Skye, not Coco . . . not anyone.'

'It's bound to hurt,' Charlotte says. 'But . . . Honey will cope. She is stronger than she thinks. She'll come round.'

Not in this lifetime, I think.

'I'll tell her I'm sorry,' I say. 'Once she's calmed down a

little bit. I am sorry, you know . . . about Shay, about Honey, about the lies . . . everything.'

'I know,' Charlotte sighs. She ruffles my hair, and I want to cry because I don't deserve her kindness, her understanding.

She opens a drawer and takes out a flat parcel wrapped in blue tissue paper and passes it to me.

'You're a creative girl, Cherry,' she says. 'You're imaginative, a dreamer. You just need to use those skills in the right way. Lies are only lies if you try to make-believe they're true . . . but what if you see them as stories, fantasies? That way you're free to imagine anything you like. You've been through a lot in your short life, Cherry . . . you're still making sense of it all. I thought that writing down the stories and fantasies might help . . .'

I open the tissue paper and inside there is a book, a beautiful, blank-paged notebook with a red silk cover embroidered with cherry blossom. It's the most beautiful thing I have ever seen.

'Oh . . . but . . . thank you, Charlotte!'

'I used to keep a sketchbook on the go when I was your age,' she tells me. 'I'd put my heart and soul into those books, and you can do the same. Use it as a diary, a memory book, a place to sort the dreams out from reality. Write stories. Imagine.'

I think about what Charlotte's just said. What if I looked at things a different way? Called the lies make-believe, like Shay does? Fantasies, stories, imaginings, creative thinking . . . ways to express the feelings inside. Surely that wouldn't be shameful or sad? If I write the stories down, they might even be something to be proud of, one day.

'I will!' I promise Charlotte. 'Thank you. I can't believe you're all being so kind to me when I've been so stupid . . . when I've lied, and . . . well, worse.'

I stroke the creamy paper, blinking back tears.

'Young love doesn't last forever,' Charlotte says. 'And trust me, Cupid has rotten aim sometimes. I don't suppose you could help liking Shay . . . and who's to say things will last for the two of you anyway? It's awkward . . . but . . . well, it's not the end of the world.'

'I thought I'd wrecked everything,' I whisper. 'I thought I'd ruined it all . . . you, Dad, the wedding, the future . . .'

'It'd take a lot more than that,' Charlotte says. 'And that's a promise . . .'

'They've set a date for the wedding,' Coco whispers. 'The first of June. We're all going to be bridesmaids . . .'

'Me too?' I ask.

'Cherry, obviously, you too!' Charlotte says. She sighs. 'Look . . . I'm sorry you felt you had to lie to fit in, be a part of things, but I think I can understand why you did. We must have seemed pretty full-on, and Honey made things tough for you right from the start. I suppose you felt out of your depth. We just want you to relax, though, be yourself . . . be one of us.'

'We'll be a proper family, soon,' Skye says. 'You'll see.'

'We're a proper family now,' Charlotte corrects her. 'A piece of paper won't change that. It's the loving and caring that really count . . .'

I want to be a part of it, and I think that maybe I can be. I have a dad who loves me, a new stepmum who cares enough to make tomato soup from home-grown tomatoes and basil from the garden, and I think on reflection I like it better than the tinned sort. I have a bunch of new step-sisters, and three of them accept me, like me even. They know I am not perfect, that I have done something bad, something awful, stolen their sister's boyfriend, scared everyone half to death . . . they may not approve, but still, they are speaking to me. I think.

Then there is the fourth sister. She hated me on sight, and she still hates me, I know, but I cannot blame her for that. I would feel the same, in her shoes. I'd like to tell her that I am sorry, that I tried and tried to stop it from happening, but I don't think she'd believe me.

I'd like to say I regret it, but I don't . . . not really.

How can I? I didn't choose Shay, and he didn't choose me. We just couldn't help it. Love is like a force of nature, something bigger than either of us, having a laugh at our expense, stirring up trouble and watching the fallout shake down.

'Shay is grounded,' Skye whispers. 'For the rest of the holidays. You should have seen his dad, last night, though . . . he yelled and he swore and then he sat at our kitchen table and cried, and Shay's mum told him he was too hard on Shay, and he said that maybe he was . . .'

I think that things might be better now, for Shay. I hope so.

It is dusk when I go outside again. I sit down by the fish pond, throw a pinch of food to Rover. Five goldfish rise up to the surface, flicking their tails, swooping and splashing, and at first I can't tell which one is Rover. Everything

✿✿✿✿✿✿✿✿✿✿✿✿✿✿✿✿✿✿✿✿✿✿✿✿✿✿

changes, I realize, but sometimes the changes are for the better. My lonely goldfish has friends now, and a pond with water lilies and a future.

'I probably won't see Shay again until September,' I tell Rover. 'When school starts. That'll be fun . . . a brand-new high school with only Honey for company . . . I'm guessing I'll be popular, right? Well, I suppose that's nothing new . . .'

Rover glides beneath a lily pad and reappears, eyeing me darkly.

'Shay will be there too, though,' I sigh. 'I won't be on my own.'

I stand up and walk across the grass, into the trees, towards the caravan, and at the last moment I look back towards Tanglewood House.

Up in the turret room, a small, slender figure is curled up on the window seat, her long Rapunzel hair fluttering a little in the breeze from the open window.

Honey is watching me, a princess in her tower, waiting for a prince who will never come. As I watch, she wipes a hand across her eyes, pushes the window wider still. I think for a minute she might call out, talk to me, yell at me, but then I see the glint of silver in her hands.

My heart stops and my eyes open wide.

The scissors slide open and shut again with a cold, crisp snip.

Slowly, slowly, slender hanks of soft, blonde hair drift down from the open window, long ribbons of gold that swirl and spiral and land like snow on the gravel drive. It goes on for five, maybe ten minutes, and when she puts the scissors down, Honey's beautiful hair is short, stark, shorn, like a prisoner or a cancer patient. Her eyes hook on to mine, a long, meaningful look, and my heart turns over.

My gaze slides away. The light is fading now, and in the lower rooms, the lights are coming on. I can hear the warm buzz of chat from the kitchen, a flicker of movement behind a curtain in one of the guest rooms, music, life.

I turn and pick my way across the grass, beneath the cherry trees, towards the little red caravan.

Read on to sample the next
scrumptious book in
the chocolate box girls
series . . .
MARSHMALLOW
SKYE

I don't believe in ghosts.

I do believe in creaky floorboards and sudden cool draughts and eerie howling sounds when the wind whistles through the eaves, because when you live in a big, old house like Tanglewood those things are part of the deal.

The house actually looks like it could be haunted. Ivy clings to the soft red brick and the windows are tall and arched and criss-crossed with lead, the kind of windows where you might expect to see a face watching you: a pale, sad-eyed shadow from the past. The sort of thing you read about in books – stories where the clock strikes twelve and you wake up to mystery and intrigue and people in rustling dresses who walk right through you as if you're not there at all.

I used to wish for something like that to happen to me. I wanted to step into the past, see it for myself. I've grown up listening to ghost stories, spent summers with my sisters, hunting for spooky visions and ghostly apparitions . . . but I have never seen a single one.

The only ghosts I believe in now are the Halloween variety: small and sticky-faced and dressed in white sheeting, clutching plastic bags full of toffee apples and penny chews.

'Skye! Summer!' my sister Coco yells, sticking her head round the door. 'Aren't you two ready yet? Cherry's downstairs waiting and I've been ready for ages too, and if we don't get a move on we'll miss the party! Hurry *up*!'

'Relax,' Summer says, scooshing her perfect hair with a blast of lacquer. 'We've got tons of time, Coco. It doesn't start until seven! Go duck for apples or something!'

'Skye, tell her!' my little sister wails. 'Make her hurry up!'

It is hard to take Coco seriously, though, because she has painted her face green, blacked out some of her teeth and spiked up her hair with neon gel. She is wearing a tweedy old jacket that belongs to Mum's boyfriend, Paddy, and I think she is supposed to be Frankenstein's monster.

'Ten minutes,' I promise. 'We'll be down soon!'

Coco rolls her eyes and stomps off down the stairs.

Summer laughs. 'She is sooo impatient!'

'She's excited,' I tell my twin. 'We used to be like that, remember?'

'We're still like that, Skye,' Summer says, smoothing down her raggedy white dress. 'Just don't tell Coco! I love Halloween, don't you? It's so cool . . . like being a kid again!'

I smile. 'I know, right?'

And Summer does know, of course . . . she knows me better than anyone else in the world. She knows how I feel about a whole bunch of things, because most of the time she feels the same.

And dressing up . . . well, that's one thing we both love.

I lean in towards the mirror, pick up a brush. I am not as good with hair and make-up as my twin, but I love the magic – the moment when you glance up and see, just for a split-second, a whole different person.

The girl in the mirror is pale and ghostly. There are ink-dark smudges beneath her wide blue eyes as if she hasn't slept for a week, and her hair is tangled and wild, twined with fronds of ivy and black velvet ribbon.

She looks like a girl from long ago: a girl with a story, a

secret. She's the kind of girl who could make you believe in ghosts.

'Awesome,' I say, grinning, and the ghost-girl grins too.

'You look gorgeous,' Summer says, and I turn away from the mirror. 'Think you'll hook up with some cute vampire boy at the party?'

'Vampire boys are a pain in the neck,' I say and Summer laughs, but the truth is that neither of us have boyfriends. We are still at the stage of dreaming about boys in books, boys in movies, boys in bands. I like it that way, and I think Summer does too.

Besides, if you saw the boys at Exmoor Park Middle School, you would understand. They are childish and annoying and definitely not crush material. Like Alfie Anderson, the class clown, who still thinks it's funny to flick chips around the canteen and set off stink bombs in the school corridor.

Classy.

Summer is perched on the edge of her bed, stroking silver sparkles along her cheekbones, painting her lips to match. Our dresses are the same: skirts made from frayed, layered strips of net, chiffon and torn-up sheets, stitched hastily on to old white vest tops.

On Summer, this looks effortlessly beautiful. On me, it looks slightly crazy and deranged. When I look back at the mirror I can see that I was fooling myself. I am not a ghost-girl, just a kid playing dress-up – and not quite as well as my sister.

I guess that is the story of my life.

Summer and I are identical twins. Mum actually has a scan from when she was pregnant, where the two of us are curled up together inside her, like kittens, and it looks like we are holding hands. The picture is fuzzy and grey, like a TV screen when the signal is lousy and everything looks crackly and broken up, but still, it's the most amazing image.

Summer came into the world first, a whole four minutes ahead of me: dazzling, daring, determined to shine. I followed after: pink-faced and howling.

They washed us and dried us and wrapped us in matching blankets and placed us in Mum's arms, and what was the first thing we did? You got it. We held hands.

That's the way it has always been, really. We were like two sides of the same coin – mirror-image kids, each a perfect reflection of the other.

Right from the start, we each knew what the other

was thinking. We finished each other's sentences, went everywhere together, shared hopes and dreams, as well as toys and food and clothes and friends. We were each other's best friend. No – more than that. We were each other.

'Aren't they gorgeous?' people would say. 'Aren't they the sweetest things you ever saw in your life?'

And Summer would squeeze my hand and tilt her head to one side, and I'd do the same, and we'd laugh and roll our eyes and run away from the adults, back to our own little world.

For the longest time, I didn't know just where Summer ended and I began. I looked at her to know what I was feeling, and if she was smiling, I smiled too. If she was crying, I'd wipe away her tears and put my arms round her, and wait for the ache inside to fade.

It sounds cheesy, but if she was hurting, I hurt too.

I thought it would be that way forever, but that's not the way it's working out.

We both went to ballet class back then – we were ballet crazy. We had pink ballet bags with little pink ballet pumps and pink scrunchies, books full of ballet stories, and a whole

box at home filled with tutus and fairy wings and wands. Looking back, I think I always liked the dressing up bit more than the actual dancing, but it took me a while to see that I was only crazy about ballet because Summer was. I saw her passion for it, and I thought I felt it too . . . but really I was just a mirror-girl, reflecting my twin.

I was fed up with ballet exams where Summer got distinctions and I struggled to scrape a pass; fed up with dance shows where Summer had a leading role while I was hidden away at the back of the chorus. She had a talent for dance, I didn't . . . and, bit by bit, it was chipping away at my confidence.

'I don't think I want to go to ballet any more,' I told Summer.

She didn't get it, though. 'You can't stop, Skye!' she argued. 'It's because you're upset about Dad leaving, isn't it? You love ballet!'

'No,' I told her. 'And this has nothing to do with Dad. *You* love ballet, Summer. Not *me*.'

Summer had a point, though. When Dad left, everything in the world turned upside-down, and messing up one more thing didn't seem to be such a big deal.

She looked at me with her face all crumpled and confused, like she didn't understand the whole idea of *you* and *me*. Well, I was just getting to grips with it myself. Up until then, it had always been *us*.

Lately, I have been wondering if that whole dancing thing might just have been the start of it. Sometimes, when you change one thing, the whole pattern falls apart, shattered, like the little pieces in a kaleidoscope. I guess I shook things up between my twin and me, and three years on we are still waiting for things to settle.

I turn back to the mirror, and for a moment I see the ghost-girl again, wild hair and sad, haunted eyes, lips parted as though she is trying to tell me something.

Then she is gone.

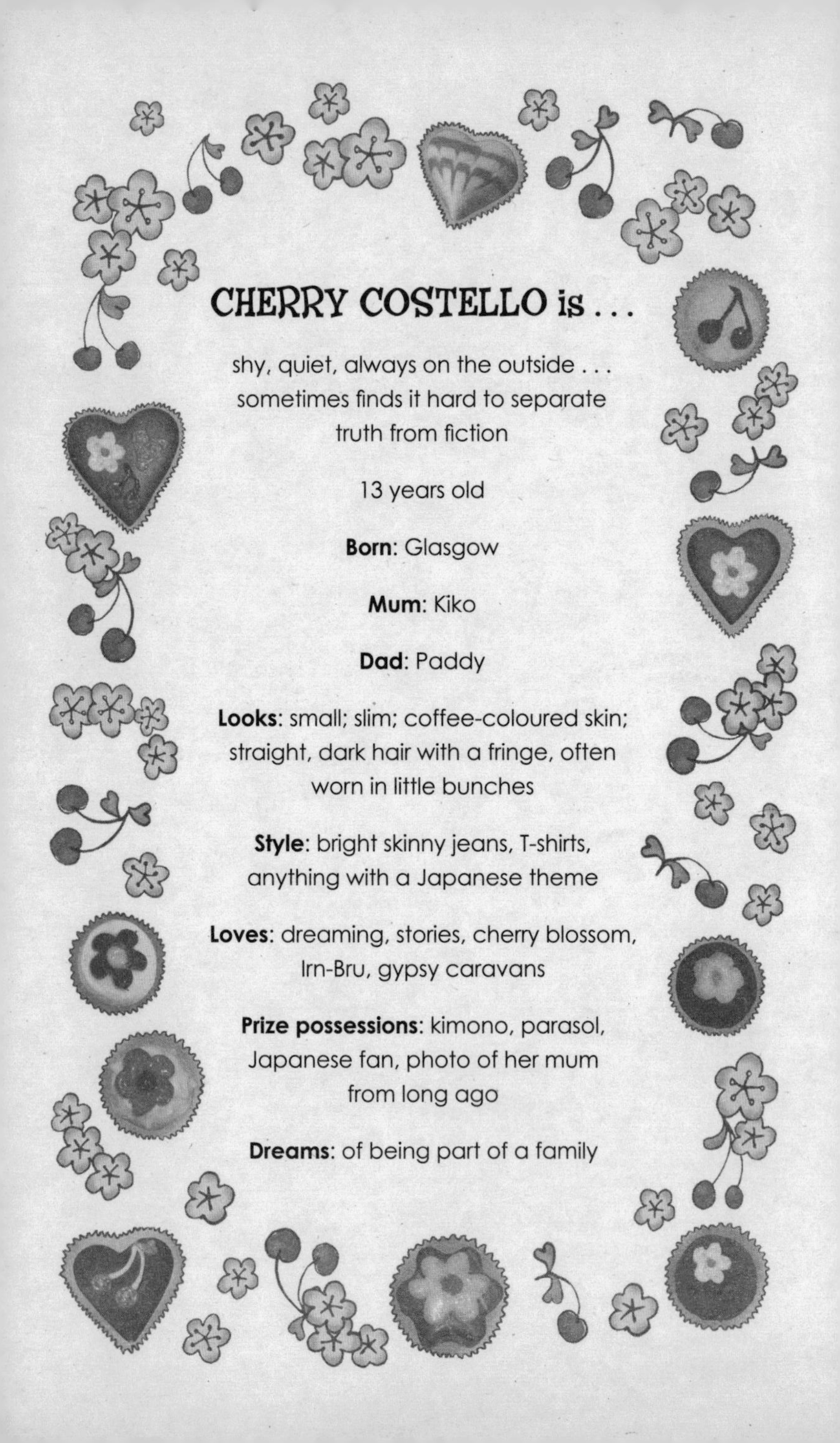

CHERRY COSTELLO is . . .

shy, quiet, always on the outside . . .
. . . sometimes finds it hard to separate
truth from fiction

13 years old

Born: Glasgow

Mum: Kiko

Dad: Paddy

Looks: small; slim; coffee-coloured skin; straight, dark hair with a fringe, often worn in little bunches

Style: bright skinny jeans, T-shirts, anything with a Japanese theme

Loves: dreaming, stories, cherry blossom, Irn-Bru, gypsy caravans

Prize possessions: kimono, parasol, Japanese fan, photo of her mum from long ago

Dreams: of being part of a family

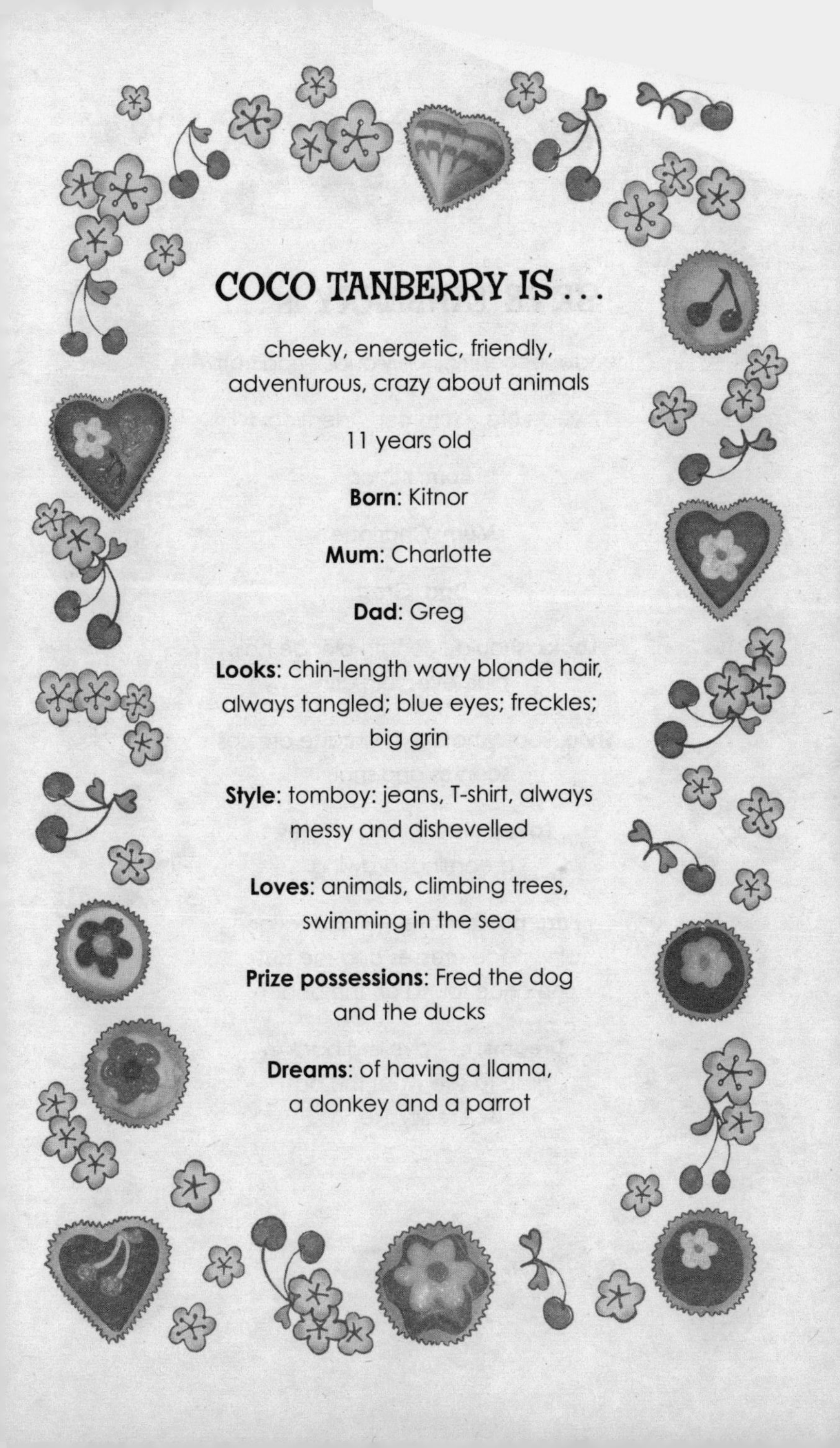

COCO TANBERRY IS . . .

cheeky, energetic, friendly, adventurous, crazy about animals

11 years old

Born: Kitnor

Mum: Charlotte

Dad: Greg

Looks: chin-length wavy blonde hair, always tangled; blue eyes; freckles; big grin

Style: tomboy: jeans, T-shirt, always messy and dishevelled

Loves: animals, climbing trees, swimming in the sea

Prize possessions: Fred the dog and the ducks

Dreams: of having a llama, a donkey and a parrot

SKYE TANBERRY is . . .

friendly, eccentric, individual, imaginative

12 years old – Summer's identical twin

Born: Kitnor

Mum: Charlotte

Dad: Greg

Looks: shoulder-length blonde hair, blue eyes, big grin

Style: floppy hats and vintage dresses, scarves and shoes

Loves: history, horoscopes, dreaming, drawing

Prize possessions: her collection of vintage dresses and the fossil she once found on the beach

Dreams: of travelling back in time to see what the past was really like . . .

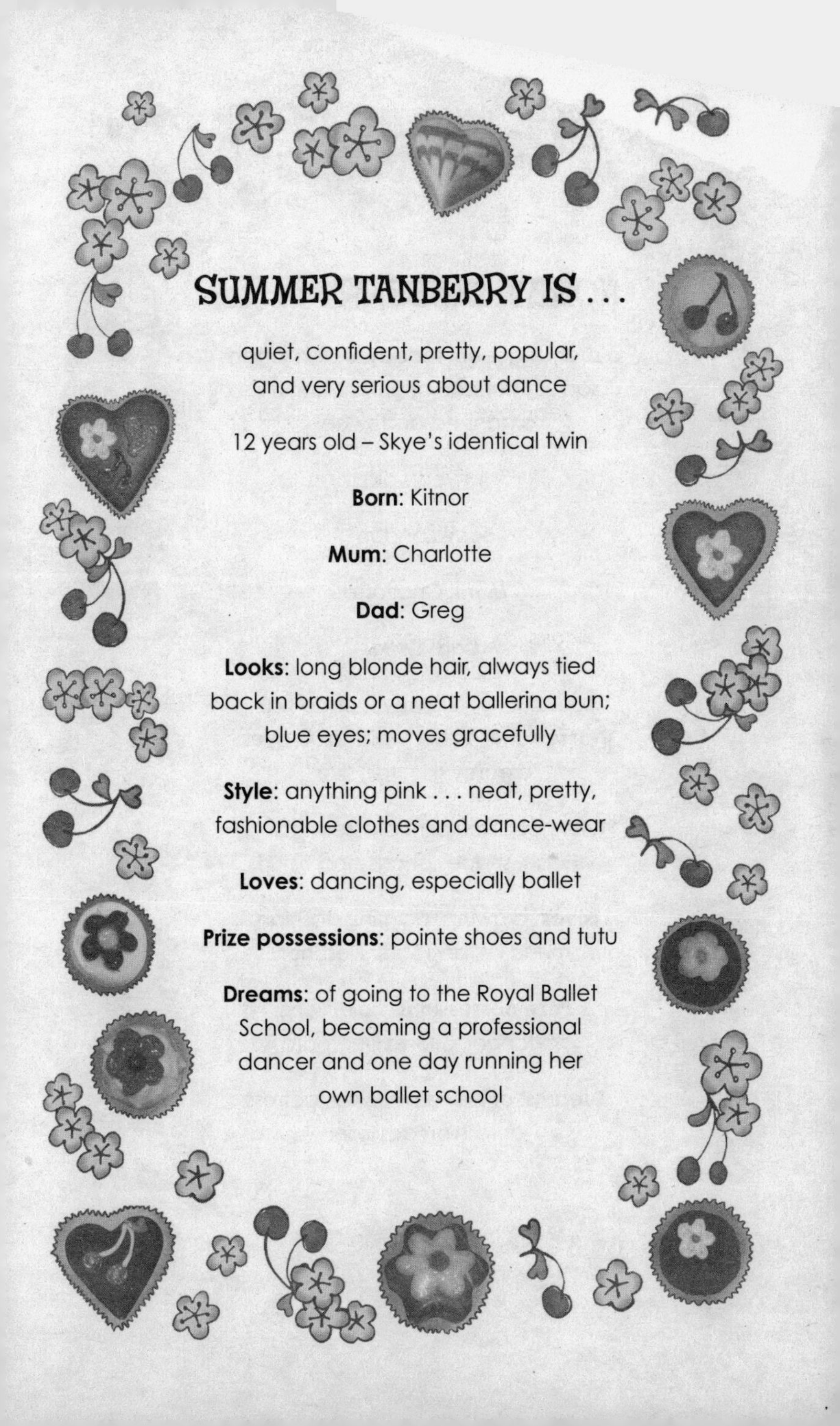

SUMMER TANBERRY IS . . .

quiet, confident, pretty, popular, and very serious about dance

12 years old – Skye's identical twin

Born: Kitnor

Mum: Charlotte

Dad: Greg

Looks: long blonde hair, always tied back in braids or a neat ballerina bun; blue eyes; moves gracefully

Style: anything pink . . . neat, pretty, fashionable clothes and dance-wear

Loves: dancing, especially ballet

Prize possessions: pointe shoes and tutu

Dreams: of going to the Royal Ballet School, becoming a professional dancer and one day running her own ballet school

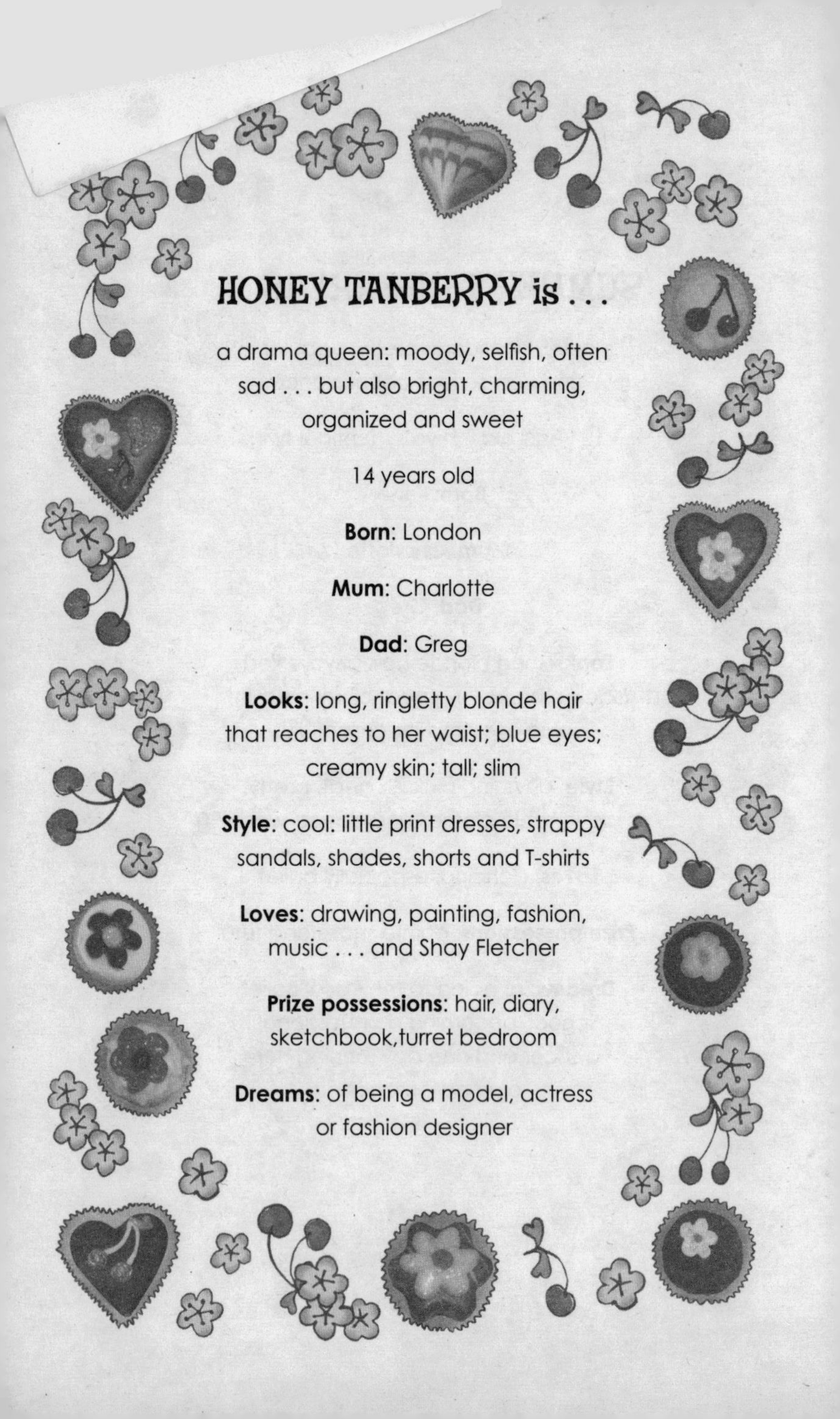

HONEY TANBERRY is . . .

a drama queen: moody, selfish, often sad . . . but also bright, charming, organized and sweet

14 years old

Born: London

Mum: Charlotte

Dad: Greg

Looks: long, ringletty blonde hair that reaches to her waist; blue eyes; creamy skin; tall; slim

Style: cool: little print dresses, strappy sandals, shades, shorts and T-shirts

Loves: drawing, painting, fashion, music . . . and Shay Fletcher

Prize possessions: hair, diary, sketchbook,turret bedroom

Dreams: of being a model, actress or fashion designer

Here's where
it all started
in Cathy's
notebook . . .

Cherry Crush
PARASOL
KIMONO
FAN...
Cherry blossom time...
secrets + lies...
Shay Fletcher - a boy who belongs to somebody else...
never knowing where you belong...
Sakura/ Cherry Costello

Which Chocolate Box Girl Are You?

Your perfect day would be spent . . .

a) visiting a busy vintage market
b) with your favourite canine companion on a long walk in the countryside
c) curled up on the sofa watching black-and-white movies with your boyfriend
d) window-shopping with your BFF
e) sipping frappuccinos in a hip city cafe

Your ideal boy is . . .

a) arty and sensitive
b) boy? No thanks!
c) a good listener . . . and a little bit quirky
d) polite and clever
e) good looking and popular – what other kind of boy is there?

Who's the first person you would tell about your new crush?

a) your sister – she knows everything about you
b) your pet cat . . . animals are great listeners
c) your BFF
d) your mum – she always has the best advice
e) no one. It's best not to trust anyone with a secret

Your favourite subject is . . .

a) history
b) science
c) creative writing
d) French
e) drama

Your school books are . . .

a) covered in paisley-print fabric
b) a bit muddy
c) filled with doodles
d) neat, tidy and full of good grades
e) rarely handed in on time

When you grow up you want to be . . .

a) an interior designer
b) a vet
c) a writer
d) a prima ballerina
e) famous

People always compliment your . . .

a) individuality. If anyone can pull it off you can!
b) caring nature – every creature deserves a bit of love
c) wild imagination . . . although it can get you into trouble sometimes
d) determination. Practice makes perfect
e) strong personality. You never let anyone stand in your way

Mostly As . . . *Skye*
Cool and eclectic, friends love your relaxed boho style and passion for all things quirky.

Mostly Bs . . . *Coco*
A real mother earth, but with your feet firmly on the ground, you're happiest in the great outdoors – accompanied by a whole menagerie of animal companions.

Mostly Cs . . . *Cherry*
'Daydreamer' is your middle name . . . Forever thinking up crazy stories and buzzing with new ideas, you always have an exciting tale to tell – you're allowed a bit of artistic licence, right?

Mostly Ds . . . *Summer*
Passionate and fun, you're determined to make your dreams come true . . . and your family and friends are behind you every step of the way.

Mostly Es . . . *Honey*
Popular, intimidating, lonely . . . everyone has a different idea about the 'real you'. Try opening up a bit more and you'll realize that friends are there to help you along the way.

Cathy's Gorgeous Cherry and Chocolate Cake with Chocolate Sauce

YOU WILL NEED:

2 ramekins
75g dark chocolate, melted – plus extra for serving
50g unsalted butter, melted
2 whole free-range eggs, beaten
50g caster sugar
50g plain flour
50g pitted cherries from a can, chopped
2 tbsp juice from a can of cherries
Butter, for greasing

- Place the chocolate, butter, eggs and sugar into a bowl and mix.
- Add the flour, cherries and cherry juice and mix together until smooth.
- Grease the ramekins with butter, then spoon the mixture into each until they're three-quarters full.
- Cover each ramekin with clingfilm, place in the microwave and cook on full power for 4 minutes, or until risen and cooked through.
- To serve, turn the puddings out on to plates and drizzle the melted chocolate on top.

Cherry's Cheeky Cherry and Chocolate Fudge

YOU WILL NEED:
180g dark chocolate
1 can of condensed milk
40g coarsely chopped almonds
40g chopped glacé cherries
1 tsp almond extract
Glacé cherry halves (optional)

- Take a 20cm-square tray and line it with foil.
- In a medium-size microwave-safe bowl, combine the condensed milk and the chocolate chips. Stir lightly.
- Microwave on High for 1.5 to 2 minutes or until the chocolate chips are melted and the mixture is smooth when you stir it.
- Now stir in the almonds, cherries and almond extract.
- Spread evenly in your prepared tray. Cover and chill in the fridge until firm.
- Cut into small squares and garnish with cherry halves, if you like. Share with your family and friends . . . or enjoy it all yourself!

Catch all the latest
news and gossip from
Cathy Cassidy
at
www.cathycassidy.com
Sneaky peeks at new titles
Details of signings and events near you
Audio extracts and interviews with Cathy
Post your messages and pictures
Don't Miss a Word!
Sign up to receive a FREE email newsletter
from Cathy in your inbox every month!
Go to www.cathycassidy.com